Kirkus Reviews

A magical-realist narrative follows a large, eccentric family in India—from dealing with the impoverished years after 1947 to finally solving the supernatural mystery plaguing the clan.

Thekkumthala (*Amballore House*, 2016) returns to the offbeat universe of his preceding novel with this linked family dynasty saga. A central figure in the ensemble cast is Thoma, a big, blaspheming, and blustery family man in the Indian state of Kerala.

Hotheaded and irresponsible, Thoma creates a lot of his own problems. He is a victim at the outset, robbed of his share of his clan's estate and ejected into the streets just as India wins independence. The new nation's poverty- and corruption-wracked growing pains mirror the family's chronic dysfunction . . . Like its predecessor, this seriocomic epic blends the myths and religions of several cultures . . . Thekkumthala's tone can go from childish to fairy-tale and dime-novel pulp to iridescent to Shakespearean without skipping a beat or violating the reality of the world of marvels and miseries he invokes . . .

A flavorful mix of genres and influences, especially captivating for fans of Indian storytelling.

https://www.kirkusreviews.com/book-reviews/jose-thekkumthala/amballore-thoma/

SPR

In *Amballore Thoma* by Jose Thekkumthala, fabulism twines with magic realism and surrealism as the poverty-stricken family meets werewolves, Chicken Little, Monsoon Man, an eight-armed woman, and more.

Amballore Thoma is whimsical and powerful, specifically because it weighs down the natural absurdity of surrealism with heavy notes of reality. Thoma and his wife Ann have a hard life, and many, many children, in a world that is also fantastically surreal. Despite the light tone the fabulist style suggests, the pain and loss in the story hit hard, and the novel does a fantastic job of blending lesser-known literary genres to create a world we can recognize clearly as our own. *Amballore Thoma* is a great read for fans of magical realism, fabulism, or surrealism. The book would also be a great fit for cultural studies and discussion groups, as this is such a singularly unique take on Indian life.

http://www.selfpublishingreview.com/2017/10/review-amballore-thoma-by-jose-thekkumthala/

Blueink Review

Amballore Thoma by Jose Thekkumthala

https://www.blueinkreview.com/book-reviews/amballore- thoma/

Seamlessly blending magic realism, mystery, and historical fiction, Joe Thekkumthala's second novel (after 2015's Amballore House) follows a large Indian family as it struggles with money, love, loyalty, and greed.

Set largely in Amballore, a small town "nestled along the southwest border of the Indian subcontinent and overlooking the Arabian Sea," the story begins in 1939 when Thoma and Ann marry. Thoma's rice-trading business is successful, and he buys a large plot of land to build his dream home. Although he generously lifts his extended family out of poverty, greedy siblings find a way to legally steal the land, leaving Thoma and his family destitute.

Forced to live in a cramped rental property in another town, he finds sporadic work as a day laborer, begins drinking heavily, and starts beating his wife—all while adding more children to his growing family. As the years pass and his children mature—and Thoma and Ann grow old— their dysfunctional family confronts some bizarre problems, and a few familiar ones that Thoma can't seem to escape.

The novel's strength is also its weakness: the sheer uniqueness of the story makes it a fascinating read, but the audacious fusion of disparate genre elements may turn off potential readers seeking a more familiar read. That said, the blending of mythologies—one of Thoma and Ann's offspring is a werewolf while another is the eight-armed Hindu goddess Bhadrakali incarnated—make for an unpredictable and, at times, whimsical, read.

Additionally, the author's focus on rich description throughout, especially the cultural elements of Indian life, deepen the narrative and create an immersive reading experience: "She wears [sic] gray sari and a brass ring is hanging from her lower lip... She smokes beedi and puffs out the smoke rings towards the bullocks."

Fiction fans who enjoy unusual reads will find this unique work—replete with werewolves, ghosts, and genies—as strange as it is charming. Think of it as Neil Gaiman meets Arundhati Roy. Also available in hardcover and ebook

BookLife Review

Amballore Thoma by Jose Thekkumthala

https://www.digitalpwselect.com/pwselect/booklife_february_27_2023/MobilePagedArticle.action?articleId=1860207#articleId1860207

Thekkumthala weaves the supernatural with tense familial bonds in his harrowing follow up to Amballore House. Thoma and his new bride, Ann, open the story with their 1939 wedding celebration in Amballore, India, but after losing his land and wealth to the ungrateful siblings he helped raise, Thoma and his family are forced to flee his ancestral land, leaving them poverty stricken and homeless. While India works to gain complete independence from Britain, the family wanders from rental to rental before finally settling in Mannuthy, where Thoma takes on odd jobs to survive and dreams of someday returning to Amballore.

On the surface, Thoma and Ann form a somewhat sturdy foundation for a large family down on their luck, but an undercurrent runs throughout that casts a pall on the household. Thoma's rough treatment of Ann doesn't stop her total dependence on him, though his ongoing domestic violence and alcoholism eventually spill over onto other relationships, including his explosive fights with his landlord over the unpaid rent, which end in disastrous consequences for Ann. As the family grows, so do their troubles—some of the children are born with otherworldly gifts, including twin Jaygust, whose brutal conception leads to his superhuman strength and murderous intent from the cradle.

Thekkumthala smoothly blends the many intricate storylines and neatly resolves the book's complex layers by its conclusion, scattering fragments of horror throughout the landscape of family drama. In the process, he manages to spotlight the family's loyalty despite their chaotic and destructive tendencies to fracture when money and greed take root. The constant flow of plot twists and supernatural elements (think were-wolves, phantom men, and goddesses spun into a family's daily life) are well-balanced by Thekkumthala's strong character development, resulting in an engaging and fast-paced novel that will blur genre lines and disquiet readers. Takeaway: A resonant family drama shrouded in mystery and the supernatural.

Great for fans of Sarah Rees Brennan's The Demon's Lexicon; Tashan Mehta's The Liar's Weave.

Forward / Clarion Review

Amballore Thoma by Jose Thekkumthala

In Jose Thekkumthala's novel Amballore Thoma, an Indian couple's misfortunes begin in Kerala and lead to fantastical twists.

Thoma is the brutish firstborn son of his family. When he assumes the patriarchal role, his ungrateful younger siblings, who think that they're owed more for having endured troubles, claim the family's land for themselves. Thus he and his suffering wife, Ann, leave home with their wisecracking parrot, Subashini. It's "a fall from farm to famine, grace to damnation." It's also 1947—the end of the British Raj—which increases the couple's pain over being ousted. Ann quips that they're a modern Adam and Eve as they embark on haphazard travels in exile. They and their children end up in a rental home.

Thoma's overblown personality exists in startling contrast to the family's poverty. His behavior sometimes catches up to him—as when a frustrated landlord doles out a public beating—but these moments are slapstick spectacles within the novel. He drinks and abuses Ann, who is treated as a joke despite her inner strength and indefatigable faith; in such cases, the story is farcical to its detriment, undercutting the gravity of its scenes.

Further, odd comparisons abound (a monsoon, for instance, is likened to a scene on an IMAX screen), resulting in a sense of absurdity. And the book's rapid transitions are jagged, genre- mixing turns; the story, at various times, resembles a fable, a comedy, and a horror story (a "Misery Man" takes up residence in Thoma's rental for a few pages in the latter case; it's a passing curiosity whose purpose is obscured). The story moves through the 1960s and the 1970s with speed, covering abrupt events like an encounter with a werewolf and encounters with Thoma and Ann's adult children. This mashup of scenes is eccentric.

Descriptions of everyday Indian life, from its flora to its foods, flesh the family's world out somewhat. Still, in the end, the book is too freewheeling. It draws from other stories, including that of Chicken Little, to ask intriguing questions about the role of chance in people's lives, and about their responses to it. The book devolves into a meandering tale that's prone to lengthy detours, and its literary experiments are irreverent if piquing—and ultimately satisfying, in that most people therein meet with the fates that they deserve.

In the comical historical saga Amballore Thoma, an Indian family confronts real and otherworldly hardships with panache.

Pacific Book Review

https://www.pacificbookreview.com/amballore-thoma/

Amballore Thoma is a charming story and the second edition by California based physicist, Joseph Thekkumthala. A bright and blissful wedding milieu between two lovers, Thoma and Anna, opens the curtains to an interesting pageant and gest that begs to inspire and answer queries on the balance of life through juggling tons of responsibilities, personalities, and feelings.

Ann's mother is sad about the decision to choose Thoma for her daughter in marriage and for this reason she has no certitude in the espousal. Thoma's character is disreputable in all aspects, from taunting his mother-in-law to razzing his new wife on the wedding day. His demeanor is far from decent as it brims with satire and jeer throughout the read, but unlike him, his wife Anna is the contrary. She is stoical and gentle, a character that is praiseworthy in both word and deed.

The plot revolves around their iffy marriage, hilarious promises, nonsensical jokes, and life's uncertainties ranging from fist fights with siblings who want a share of Thoma's wealth that he industriously worked hard to acquire, to siring innumerable children whose names the couple has interestingly no cognizance of. Attempts by the protagonist to take matters into his own hands only land him into misery and eviction through a harsh court verdict that leaves him and his wife begging for shelter and food.

Things exacerbate further when a rather spooky and uninvited guest forces his way into his house, sending Thoma's family into a frozen state. The scene is likened to having a slithering reptile in the house that won't back down without a fight. A man who will tussle anyone including his landlord, and one who blames his wife for everything including the existence of biting insects is about to have it rough with this callous assailant. Readers won't wait to masticate through the chapters of this riveting tale that grips from beginning to end, through striking narration and terrific recital that dazzles, laced with clever quotes from famous writers that add depth and continuity to an alluring plot.

Thekkumthala's writing style is original and pleasant, as flaunted by the clear-cut language that fits so well into this book's genre and pattern. It is a five-star publication with a well-developed setting, a thought-provoking and entertaining motif, drawing to a satisfying conclusion that confirms the author's tour de force creative and writing skills

Amballore Thoma Book Review by **US Review of Books**

https://www.theusreview.com/reviews-1/Amballore-Thoma-by-Jose-Thekkumthala.html

*"Coffin dodger is Gang's nickname for Thoma, coined
for his unpardonable crime of being alive and keeping
at it. They would rather he quit doing that."*

After their arranged marriage, Thoma and Ann seem to be living the good life when it all falls to pieces. The couple lose Thoma's parental home and property to his younger siblings, whom Thoma had been raising. They become homeless and bounce from place to place until they eventually settle in a rental which includes a cruel landlord.

Ann does her best to make their little rental a home and provides Thoma with ten children, one of whom is the landlord's through rape. This child, like the landlord, is a werewolf. Thoma works odd jobs, drinks too much, and sometimes hits Ann.

His older children are dutiful and driven to get out and make their own way in life. The younger children don't think their parents do enough and expect more from them. The family is visited by a variety of spirits and Indian mythological beings, which play important roles in the family narrative.

Thekkumthala has written an interesting book which is both a family saga and a glimpse into the magical world of Indian gods and myths. The writing is crisp. Thekkumthala often writes quotable phrases through his wordplay.

The fantastical elements of the book really bring the narrative to life. This is especially beneficial in a work like this, where the protagonist is not entirely likable or likely to inspire too much empathy. Those familiar with magical realism in works by Isabel Allende or Gustavo Patriau will find a similar offering.

JOSE THEKKUMTHALA

AMBALLORE THOMA

Published in the United States of America

Brilliant Books Literary
137 Forest Park Lane Thomasville
North Carolina 27360 USA

ISBN:
Paperback: 979-8-88945-495-3
Ebook: 979-8-88945-496-0

To: Jennifer, Lisa, and April.

CONTENTS

ONE

FROM RICHES TO RAGS

May this wedding bliss spread from now on to evening of your lives.

The priest announces in a stunning voice, deep and profound. He has a funeral voice—grave and tinged with sadness, hardly the voice suiting a wedding ceremony and yet it draws the attention of the parishioners inside Amballore Cathedral.

The crowd cheers for Thoma and Ann, the groom, and the bride. Ann's face brightens with beaming smile; Thoma has a serious look. They stand a few feet from the altar. The year is 1939.

"Thoma, what is *evening of life*?" Ann leans toward Thoma, stands on her toes to reach his ears, and whispers. She is barely five feet tall and Thoma towers over her with his impressive height.

He doesn't have an answer. To be caught with no answer to his wife-to-be's query belittles his masculine pride. So, he makes up one.

"Your *mother's ass*—that's what *evening of life* is."

The cathedral is rocked by a thunder-like roar of laughter. Ann's face turns blood-red with embarrassment. She bows her head, and stares at the floor, counting marble tiles. Even though she inched closer to Thoma for fear of being overheard and murmured in his ear, he answered in his booming voice tinged with sarcasm and irritation. The voice needed no loudspeakers to be broadcast.

The only evening Ann knows is the widely understood evening in a day, when husbands return home from a hard day's work and wives prepare supper. All India Radio broadcasts news and plays Malayalam movie songs. The appetizing aromas of fried fish and boiled tapioca fill the air.

Somewhere in the distance, someone is playing devotional hymns too loud not to take notice of. The sun, the workaholic of the day, paints itself orange and red prior to taking a dip in the Arabian Sea for a much-needed evening bath. That is the kind of evening she knows, not the evening of life.

Little did Ann know that *your mother's ass* is staple of Thoma's phraseology. He uses it indiscriminately. As married life unfolds, she gets the sneaking suspicion that one day he would engrave it on a granite rock, save it, and use it as her tombstone when she dies.

The bridesmaid Theresa, Ann's younger sister, stands nearby, laughing her head off when her to-be brother-in-law publicizes her mother's bottom. The trumpet flowers on her hair shake wildly when she laughs, threatening to fall off any moment.

Varghese Mappila, Ann's father, is present in the crowd, whose earth- shattering orgasm resulted in Ann's birth twenty-three years ago, an event that defied the laws of probability. You see, Ann wasn't supposed to be born, since it violates the law of *Survival of the Fittest*.

Ann's mother, Rosy, is in attendance too, glued to her husband and head bent in deep prayer, unaware of the commotion created by her future son-in-law. The audience take a quick peek at Rosy's bottom, only to realize that it isn't something to write home about. Rosy is a noodle-thin woman with a flat ass—not much to look at.

Rosy prays for the safety of her dear daughter in married life. She has deep misgivings on choosing Thoma as her daughter's husband in an arranged marriage set-up. However, her protests go unheeded by the patriarch, Varghese who decides Thoma is the right fit for Ann.

Thoma is six feet tall. His hair is long, touching the shoulders. He takes after his mother, Eli, who is tall and endowed with intimidating personality. With a muscular body, good looks, and sumptuous hair, he is often mistaken for a Malayali movie actor. He is elegantly dressed, sporting a moustache and a cleanly shaven face. After dropping the nuclear bomb, he appears to have a casual look, seemingly unaware of the attention his words invited.

His younger brother Inasu, the best man, stands by him with an equally serious face.

Ann, a humble and unassuming woman, has finely defined features.

Amballore citizens believe that God created Ann when he was taking geometry lessons. His project was to create a geometry-themed female. He sure enough created such one with perfect symmetry—cylindrical neck, circular eyes, triangular chin, and rectangular forehead. However, she lacked aesthetic merit, as God belatedly realized. By then it was too late for alterations; it was time to submit the project. "Symmetry does not translate into beauty," the teacher scribbled on God's project report and gave him a B minus.

Ann is adorned with suspended ear-rings huge like church bells. Her long flowing hair hosts a garland of marigold flowers. She has a golden necklace which sparkles in the light from the ornamental chandeliers hanging above. Her parents gifted it as her dowry.

Monsoon raindrops splatter on the roof and their tup-tup-tup sound becomes distinct. It is a rainy day in July, not cloudy-dark, but faintly sunny. The crowd arrived carrying rain-soaked umbrellas dripping wet, creating an instant swimming pool inside the cathedral.

The sunlight streams through the cathedral's multi-colored stained glass and becomes a rainbow of colors falling straight on Varghese's crystal-clear bald head. The reflected light blinds the parishioners; they squint to see the bride and the groom, the celebrities of the occasion.

"This marriage is made in heaven." The priest intones. "May it not be broken by the mortals; God has willed it."

He sneezes so loudly at the end of the pronouncement that the seven- year-old flower girl drops the bouquet involuntarily and the four-year-old screams louder than the sneeze and runs to her mom's lap.

The man of God then declares the couple husband and wife.

After marriage, Thoma faces many more questions from Ann. He becomes her source of information on everything—except matters of the Church. He is an atheist and can't help her there. She asks questions out of the simpleminded curiosity with which she is abundantly endowed, barely realizing she is baring her common sense–starved brain to the scrutiny of the world.

She learns that Thoma has a vast vocabulary of words, expressions, and phrases she was unaware of. She admires him for his general knowledge.

She takes note when Thoma uses the expression *burden of life* while grumbling about the responsibilities that his father and mother entrusted with him in bringing up his siblings. Is *burden of life* heavier than the haystacks she carries on her head during harvest season? She wonders, but decides not to ask in case he decides to shower her with profanities. She keeps remembering what he said on their wedding day.

Irrespective of Thoma's out-of-the-norm behavior, he is the rock on which Ann leans. His word is her Bible. She enjoys asking him about their future, which Thoma is eager to answer. He is a big dreamer, building castles in the air, and giving her ungrounded promises about the golden life they would ultimately embrace.

"Thoma, when will we board the rainbow as you promised?" Ann asks.

On their wedding night, he promised they would sail together along a rainbow to reach a pot of gold.

"Just stick with me; you'll be there before you know it," he says, shedding a rare smile. Ann salivates, inspired by the wise saying from the prophet Thoma. He lights up a beedi and takes couple of puffs. "I'll take you to the Promised Land as certainly as the earth is round."

For the first time, Ann learns that the earth is round. All along, she believed it is flat. "Is the earth round, Thoma?" she asks on the spur of the moment, forgetting the risks of asking him questions. As soon as he turns to her with his restless eyes twinkling with mischief, she knows she is in trouble. While he is readying to answer, she realizes that another *mother's ass* is on its way from his sarcastic mouth. She looks away, realizing it is too late to take back the question, and moves out of his arm swing's range in case he decides to grace her with one of his notorious beatings. She remembers being battered like rice flour on occasions like this when her questions irritated him.

"Earth is flat like your mother's ass," Subashini, the family's pet parrot, says. She is sitting in her cage hanging above, listening to the conversation and eating peanuts.

Thoma smiles approvingly. Ann feels that Thoma is speaking through his beloved parrot.

"Thoma, even though you are now married, you must still love your siblings as though they are your own children," Vareed, Thoma's dad, says. "Keep my advice carved in stone and store it in a corner of your heart. Let it be a guiding principle now and always, even after Eli and I are dead and gone."

Thoma is the eldest son of Vareed and Eli. The family has six boys and three girls altogether. They lived in a small town called Amballore in the state of Kerala, nestled along the southwest corner of the Indian subcontinent and overlooking the Arabian Sea.

One of the boys, Raphael, committed suicide by kissing his head goodbye and donating it to a train that came hurtling down the rail tracks. This happened in the year 1947. He was twenty-five years old. He had been caught in the crosshairs of a star-crossed love affair.

"I have tired old bones and am hanging up the hat," Vareed says. "You're young and energetic; be their savior and earn their gratitude."

By this time, Thoma has been married and has three children. He is still living at his parental home, taking care of his wife and children and the extended family. After marriage, luck turns in his favor. He successfully builds a rice-trading business, buying rice on wholesale and selling it to retailers. The proceeds are used to buy a large piece of real estate. He builds a home on the newfound land. "This is our promised land," He tells Eli with pride.

The town folks know that Thoma lifted the extended family from the quagmire of poverty they inherited, breathing life into their lives, and giving them freedom and dignity. Ann knew from the very beginning of the marriage that Thoma is the guard dog of the family, unwaveringly devoted to it. Eli knows that her eldest son is consumed with a passionately dogged determination to pull his siblings out of the lot they were born into.

A day arrives when his siblings demand their share of the property. "You can't demand property," Thoma says. "I bought it out of my sweat and blood; it doesn't outflow from previous generations."

"You are like our own father to us." They play to his finer sense of compassion. "Whatever belongs to you belongs to us too."

If he is going to share the property, it is out of the goodness of his heart, so thinks Ann. For his indisputable sacrifice for his siblings, they should reward him with gratitude instead of squeezing the very last rupee out of him, so went her thought process. Instead, they file a case against him in Amballore Court. The court passes the judgment that annuls Thoma's property ownership.

"The court hereby removes defendant's rights to his ancestral property," read the judgment order. "Our decision is based upon the evidence presented by the plaintiff in the form of a document promising them his share of the land."

The defendant is Thoma and the plaintiff his siblings.

During the proceedings leading to the judgment, Thoma is outraged upon seeing the document his siblings present. He knows right away it is fraudulent. It is a proverbial backstab. "You can shove your document," he says to his siblings while judge is presiding and storms out of the court, indignation writ large on his face.

"Where is the promised gratitude, Father?" Thoma asks Vareed. "Didn't you promise they would be grateful to me always?" Vareed gropes for an answer, looking away from his son.

Thoma, looking like a deranged man, barges into his now-estranged home brandishing a weapon of destruction—a gleaming sickle. His siblings smell trouble as soon as they spot Thoma with a vacant stare marching toward them. He has unsteady steps, being drunk on toddy. He wobbles like a spinning top and lurches on. He is consumed with a single-minded determination to exterminate his thankless siblings.

They take to their heels, never taking second chance with him. Thoma swiftly follows them, but they outrun. They climb to the roof of the farmhouse and pull the ladder off the ground before he approaches. They huddle together on the roof, hiding in plain sight—with unadulterated fear that their heads would be on the chopping block if they get any closer to him. The outmaneuvered Thoma is stranded on the ground.

The land around their home is spacious. It is a two-acre ranch housing the family home, a barn, and a pasture. The cows are feeding in the pasture. The chickens, ducks, and goats roam freely. Coconut palms fill the yard, giving it a look of paradise.

"I dare you to come down and fight like men." His booming voice assaults his siblings' ears. Terrified ducks quack on endlessly. Amid the mooing of the cows and squealing of the pigs, Thoma curses his siblings and drops the sickle. He is like Mahatma Gandhi embracing nonviolence—only because he has no other choice.

But not so fast!

As soon as Thoma turns around to head for home, he spots Agasty, his brother, frantically climbing a coconut palm to escape him. Thoma follows Agasty up the tree like an agile monkey and catches up with him halfway to the top. The brothers wrestle. The slender palm oscillates like a pendulum.

While the family watches this alarming scene from the roof, the palm snaps, disembarking the men who'd violated her slender body like two rapists would mount a female. The tree breaks into two, dropping them on the ground. They continue to fight like two wrestlers in the heat of the moment, totally unaware they have been dropped to the ground.

Thoma gets an upper hand. He grabs Agasty's neck with his left hand, stands him up against the broken tree, and punches him repeatedly until he collapses after sustaining a bloodied head. The fallen sibling is lucky Thoma had thrown away his sickle earlier.

"Don't bite the hand that fed you," Thoma says in his thundering voice, but Agasty is way beyond hearing; he had turned unconscious.

"It applies to you cowards too." He gazes at his siblings. "This one is for you all." He then gives Agasty a hard kick—a final kick, a kick for the road. He is now ready to hit the road.

"If you ask my siblings to tell the truth at the risk of being blown to pieces otherwise, they will acknowledge they are scumbags but for me," he says to Ann.

"You went overboard helping them," Ann says. "Look at us now, we are homeless."

"Take me with you, Thoma," Subashini says. Thoma unhooks the cage and carries the bird with him. The parrot makes happy chirping sounds, spreading its red and green feathers.

Thoma leaves the ancestral property with Ann and their three children—George, Rita, and Kareena. He is thirty-seven, and Ann thirty-one. The year is 1947.

The day is historic—India gains independence from the British Raj on that day. The news that nonviolent struggle led by Mahatma Gandhi leads to its independence unfolds over the airwaves. It is unheard of for someone like Gandhi, a down-to-earth saint, to bring the mighty British Empire to its knees. The Indians suddenly become aware of their power which lay dormant for a century. The nation is seized by the fever of victory.

Widespread celebrations ensue. The fireworks in Amballore give the town a festival atmosphere.

"We're losing freedom when India is gaining hers," Ann states the obvious. The family is huddled together in a street corner and Ann fights off the August wind that tousles her long, black hair.

They soon get consigned to the prison of homelessness, becoming gypsies, migrating from village to village in search of a home. The new lifestyle is a far cry from the prodigal one they were used to. Ann knows that theirs is a precipitous fall—a fall from farm to famine, from grace to damnation.

"We've fallen from Riches to Rags," Ann says.

"Trust me," Thoma says. "Somewhere in this whole wide world, there is a home for us."

"We'll follow you to the ends of the earth," Subashini says. She is endowed with unabating cheerfulness and optimism, something the family badly needs.

"For now, we are homeless," Thoma says. "But mark my word, one day we will have a home."

Ann knows he is a big dreamer, building castles in the air.

"Any place is a home when my family is around, even if it is just an open space with no walls and roof. It will be our own open space under our own vast blue sky." Thoma makes ownership claims on earth and sky.

"We are the modern-day Adam and Eve," Ann says. "We are cast out of the Garden of Eden into the grim darkness. We're doomed, aren't we, Thoma?"

She hopes he would deny it. Instead, Thoma puffs out a smoke ring.

They end up in numerous rental homes. Some are worse than outhouses, some worse than slum dwellings and others with crumbling walls and absent roofs, resembling showpieces of a decadent civilization.

"Street life is better than these rentals," Ann says.

Thoma is unable to hold on to the rentals he lands. He has rifts with the landlords over unpaid rent. He marches from rental to rental as if getting rid of an old habit. Once settled at a new place, he would be cast out—like a termite by an exterminator or like an evil spirit by an exorcist. The family is always on the go, Thoma is leading the pack and the rest closely behind him.

They endure harsh life in the damned valley of distress, crisscrossing legions of heartless landlords, and leading nomadic life.

Ann loses count of the rentals Thoma dragged her through. She gives up keeping track of them and becomes a female Buddha, resigned to her version of the enlightenment of life—that Mother Earth is their home, and the big sky above their roof.

By the time the family is done with numerous rentals, they get acquainted with people in every nook and cranny of the wider Trichur County to which Amballore belongs. By now, Thoma knows every landlord in the county, having built uneasy tenancy through rental-contract violations. Not the kind of acquaintance prompting him to chat with them over a bottle of toddy,

The family circus, at last, lands in a town of the name Mannuthy. The wandering tribe puts an end to their biblical-like exodus in the year 1949, two years after they left Amballore. Paradoxical though it might sound, they abdicate the freedom of their street like life on that day to take up new tenancy of a decent brick and mortar building.

"Monthly rent is one hundred rupees. The pet fee for parrot is twenty- five," Chettiar, the landlord, says.

"Here is my pet fee," Subashini says with a quick poo and making fart sound. "Take my poo as fee; fart is free," she adds for good measure.

While the children break into laughter, Chettiar sends a steely look to the mocking bird, a stare so intimidating that it will stop mere mortals dead in their tracks, but Subashini is nonchalant and continues to peck on the peanuts.

"Mom, he is a bad man," Kareena says. "Let us go from here." Ann hushes her baby daughter.

Chettiar's enraged eyes dart restlessly and home in on every one of the future tenants assembled in front of him. "Be forewarned of me," his angry stare tells them. Thoma figures that his body language makes him look like a distortion of space—unlike the rest of humanity who occupies it.

The rental is the end unit of a triplex. The landlord resides at the other end in a large unit. Kumaran, the barber, and his wife, Bhavany, lease the middle unit. They live with their adolescent daughter. Thoma's rental has one spacious bedroom, a large kitchen, and an outsized front porch. It is called a shotgun house; all the rooms are in a single straight line, forcing one to go through every room to get to another—there is no connecting hallway. The design claims the name *line-room architecture*, the simplest one in the world.

Thoma and George sleep on the porch. Ann, Rita, and Kareena sleep in the bedroom immediately behind. This room duplicates as Ann's prayer room. Behind the bedroom is the kitchen. There is a water well in the side yard. An outhouse serves their toilet needs, and a shed attached to the well is the bathroom.

The attic is just above the girls' bedroom. The landlord prohibits the family from entering it under any circumstance. There is a staircase leading to it. He makes it clear not to block the stairway by cluttering it with books or other household belongings. "The staircase and the attic belong to me; they are off-limits to you. You hear?" Chettiar's lips are sealed tight after the order.

"Mom, why is he mad at us?" Rita asks.

"The madman is mad at everyone," Subashini says.

Chettiar keeps some of his belongings in the attic. He occasionally appears at the rental, enters at his will, climbs the staircase, and spends time in the attic.

"It is just an excuse for him to spy on us," Ann says. She knows it is a blatant intrusion into their lives engineered by a crafty landlord.

"The audacity of the bastard," Thoma says and spits bitterly.

The rental's backyard showcases green foliage and an abundant number of tropical trees, fruits, and nuts. Jackfruit trees, coconut palms, mango trees, and plantain trees adorn the yard. Areca nuts, cashews, pineapples, papayas, and black pepper are plentiful.

"Let us be thankful for small mercies," Ann says to Thoma, looking at the greenery. She imagines the yard as a microcosm of the tropical paradise of Kerala and as a lavish treat for the eyes and mind.

"This beauty is an elixir for the body and soul," Bhavany says to Ann.

Even though the rental unit is decent, it is a far cry from what they are used to in Amballore. Thoma was an affluent man there. In Mannuthy, he must take up several jobs to support the family. He becomes a carpenter, a fisherman, a cook, an auto-rickshaw driver—you name it.

Finally, he settles on Masonry work which often takes him to nearby towns. It is a seasonal work unavailable during the harsh rainy season of the Monsoon. The family gets resigned to the new life because they know that the beggars can't be choosers. Life has declared an open season on them.

Kumaran and Bhavany prove to be a down-to-earth couple. They orient Thoma's family to the ins and outs of the new town. Kumaran is a barber, and Bhavany a housewife. She often feeds Thoma's children in her kitchen. They get free haircuts from Kumaran.

"One day we'll be out of here; we will be free, mark my words!" Thoma says. Ann knows Thoma likes Amballore, since his ancestry is rooted there. For him, being free means getting back to Amballore.

Thoma imagines that If his dream of relocating to Amballore materializes, it would be reminiscent of the triumphant return of Napoleon to Paris from the island of Elba whereto he was excommunicated from Paris.

For now, he is away from his Paris— Amballore. In the fullness of time, he will return to his dreamland. For now, he must make do with what he has.

For now, he is on his island of Elba.

TWO

MONSOON MAN

One day, monsoon arrives. The deafening sounds of thunder and flashes of lightning enact a giant IMAX movie on the screen spread across Kerala.

The torrential rain carries hailstorm which pelts Mannuthy with cannonball-sized pellets. The dark clouds hover over the town, making the day look like dusk.

The very air feels ominous.

"Your God is on vacation," Thoma blames Ann.

He is at his rental, watching Nature's fireworks. With him is Ann and their children. Giving them company is the family's pet parrot, Subashini.

They listen to raindrops fall on the plantain leaves making tup-tup-tup sound. Palm trees sway in the wind.

"Huh?" Ann is at a loss.

"He is not picking up my call for help," Thoma, the atheist, says with sarcasm and anger which color his brownish skin with an orange reddish hew. "God is too busy enjoying human misery to pick up my call. He must be sitting in his crystal palace, far from the madding monsoon. I bet it doesn't rain where he is."

Ann's God-related conversation with Thoma has resulted in painful sideshows in the past when he beat invisible mosquitos off her face. She involuntarily massages beaten tracks on her face and watches rain-soaked ducks resting in the backyard patio, huddled and shivering in the wind. The usually noisy bunch doesn't utter a single "quack".

"Keep calling him, Thoma. One day he will pick up the phone. Never lose hope."

Her ever-present happy face overflows with an abundance of optimism. Two large, thick bronze earrings hang from her ears, their weights working their way to make the earlobes stretch, exposing progressively widening holes through which a sniper could shoot without so much as touching her ears.

"Thoma's children are hungry," Subashini announces from the cage. The bird is hungry too. Ann doesn't have peanuts to fill a little bowl in the corner of the cage.

It is a day in June. The rain brings life to a standstill. Businesses close, construction work is put on hold, and farmers take sanctuary in their homes, away from the flooded paddy fields. Money is hard to come by. Grocery stores are closed—nothing to sell. People starve.

Thoma's attempts to find masonry work, his trade, is severely cut short. He is forced to stay home. He sleeps days on end, is unable to feed his children, to clothe them, and to pay rent. There is no one to borrow money from. The children have no quality clothing. They have no umbrellas, no schoolbooks, and no lunches to carry to school. So, they skip classes.

It would take three to four months for the rain to subside. Thoma prepares for the long haul when he would count months, then weeks, and finally days before the uplifting harvest season would arrive, putting an end to the wet show. For now, life is on hold, on a standstill. He chuckles at his funny thought where God who watches human misery on a huge Kerala- wide TV presses remote's pause button to watch in close detail the hungry population spread across the land.

"Everyone, come quickly," Kareena shouts in panic. The entire family comes running. Their eyes home in on where Kareena is staring. "Look," she points her trembling index finger at a strange-looking shadow cast against the wall. They stare at the poorly lit wall. There is someone's shadow lurking in the corner underneath the window curtain. Its face stares straight at their incredulous faces.

"It is moving!" everyone says in surprise. The shadow takes out its tongue and licks its upper lip as if drinking in the raindrops that washes down its face.

"The shadow has penetrated the wall!" Rita exclaims.

The family is stunned by the incredible scene of a shadow penetrating the concrete wall and showing up inside the house. Thoma opens the window and looks outside. What he sees unsettles him. Everyone joins him around the window to see what his fearful eyes are seeing. Then they see it.

Standing outside in the front yard under the plantain tree is Monsoon Man!

Monsoon Man was carried by rainstorm and dropped in the street. He crossed the street and is now right outside the rental.

The gathered family watches him curiously, but cautiously. The many wrinkles on his leathery face makes him look one hundred years old. His commanding height gives him an imposing presence.

He has restless eyes. He is scary looking like a cobra. He has deep-set yellow eyes like a lizard's. His shoes are made of snakeskin. Fire blazes in his eyes. He has labored breathing like an asthmatic patient. His skin is pockmarked with disfiguring smallpox scars. His nostrils spew out fireballs. He snorts loudly. When he sneezes, thunderbolts erupt.

"I am here to stay the whole monsoon, my friends!" He announces while walking into the house. None in the family likes being called *friend* by a cobra-resembling beast.

His voice sounds like it is reverberating from different underground layers inside earth, as if they underwent multiple echoes off the walls of a deep canyon. The sound emanating from inside his throat undergoes a strange transformation on the way out, as if it comes from a wild animal. He fixes a grin on his lizard face. He hangs the dripping umbrella on the wooden beam of the ceiling. He then makes himself at home by sitting on an empty chair.

"You are not welcome here," Thoma says. "You have rotten teeth," Subashini adds.

Monsoon Man, also known as Hunger Man or Misery Man ignores the comments. Everyone knows he couldn't be wished away because his visit is foreordained. It is a permanent fixture of the Monsoon season, this visit of him—like the midnight-like dark days of the depressing season, like the gloom written on the faces of the toiling masses of rural Kerala, and like the starvation that stalks them during the season. Monsoon Man commands Thoma to put his livelihood on hold, effectively asking him to go to hell—to die.

Thoma and Ann realize that his visit has all the elements of a grand ceremony. It looks like a staged act. He arrives like an actor making his dramatic entrance onto center stage. He makes a spectacular entry, clad in a black robe trailing behind him signaling the black days of misery ahead. The family shudder at the sight of the strange creature.

"Please leave; you are scaring the children," Ann says. In reply, he laughs hysterically, and howls demonically.

He smokes beedi, puffing out its black smoke, fixing his stare at the leaky roof. He chews tobacco at the same time and spits out blood-red liquid at the cracked front door.

"The devil is here. Trouble ahead!" Subashini warns.

His mere presence sows discomfort in the hearts of the children; it triggers a solemn silence in an otherwise noisy home. Ann hides fearfully in the inner sanctum of her leaking kitchen, like a lamb sentenced to be killed. Her terrified heart beats out of control. It could just as well have leaped out of her chest to get away from the monsoon monster. The children take refuge inside Bhavany's home. The good neighbor feeds them and consoles them.

The assembled chickens in the yard crows non-stop upon seeing the intimidating demon. The stray dog that sneaks into Ann's kitchen through the hole in the door is scared stiff. It howls with fear and runs away with its tail tucked between its hind legs.

Thoma doesn't have a bona fide cigarette or even a beedi. The tobacco had alleviated the pain of hunger; it had helped put out the fire in his belly. But now, he doesn't even have it. He smokes handcrafted beedi made of newspaper scrapped from the street.

"This will do you good," Monsoon man tosses a beedi to Thoma. "Let us celebrate the Monsoon by smoking."

"Is the gift a gesture of friendship and an attempt at cordiality?" Thoma asks himself, concluding that the man may be, just maybe, not bad after all.

"I'm a special guest to your special family," the Misery Man reminds. "Remember, I don't visit anyone else."

Special family! The ridicule is piercing like a spell of chilly down-pour. But then it is true that Monsoon Man doesn't visit anyone else. Thoma's family is special to him.

"Cut out the sarcasm," Thoma admonishes while puffing out beedi smoke.

"Let us make a toast. Let us drink to monsoon, my friend." Misery Man retrieves a toddy bottle from his black bag.

They drink together. Thoma accepts the uninvited guest's philanthropic gestures despite their mocking undercurrents. He has no other choice except to be at the receiving end of the insults. He is hungry, miserable, and lonesome, and any company is welcome to see him through the depressing season. He would have even befriended the devil just to get through the monsoon. He would have shared toddy with Lucifer. He swallows his pride and drinks.

He, however, wishes that the stranger doesn't address him as *my* friend.

The Misery Man has detailed plans. He makes sure that Ann has no rice to cook the whole season, that firewood to fuel the clay oven becomes scarce, and that the pots and pans remains unwashed since there is no cooking. He makes sure that Thoma is out of a job, ousting his ability to feed his children. He makes sure the children's school dues aren't paid and that the family can't buy blankets to withstand the cold monsoon. He makes sure that the family catches the aroma of fried fish from its neighbors' kitchens, revamping the ache of hunger. He makes sure there are skirmishes with the landlord over the unpaid rent. He makes sure that the kerosene could not be bought to light up the lamp, forcing the children to read under the streetlamps with umbrellas held overhead. He makes sure the roof leaks, creating an indoor swimming pool. He makes sure misery reigns supreme.

His grand plan includes every pathetic detail that starves the body and weakens the spirit.

"I don't mind starving," Ann says when streaks of faint sunlight cast by the afternoon sun brightens her kitchen. "But I can't live with my dispirited soul."

Halfway through his visit Monsoon Man undergoes a dramatic change. Subashini notices it first. The transformation is gradual, but definite.

"Look—the devil has a new head," she chirps from the cage.

Everyone shoots a glance at him. Sure enough, they see another head growing near his head. As the days progress, the second head grows bigger and the original head smaller. The children call the original head "monsoon head" and the newly sprouted head "harvest head."

"Hail to the harvest head," they cheer and scream, rooting for the new head.

The monsoon head becomes diminutive and looks starved. It still shows its vicious and twisted frown. His other head—the head that holds the promise of harvest—became energized. It holds out the promise of the Onam festival that arrives sometime after the monsoon.

And then one day, one of the last rainfalls of the season arrives. The season is mercifully reaching its end, the family realizes with relief.

Monsoon Man prepares to leave, immensely satisfied at sowing terror in the family. He has brought down the self-esteem of everyone to the lowest level. He spits wildly at the cracked door and tosses another beedi to Thoma.

This gesture had marked his arrival, and now it marks his departure.

Before departing he beckons Thoma to his side and makes a promise to come back. "I'll be back next rainy season, my friend!" his emaciated monsoon head says. Thoma once again cringes at being called *my friend*.

"Don't call me *my friend*," Thoma says.

"Be sure you are at home when I arrive next time, my friend! Remember, I like you." He rubs salt in the wounds.

Just before taking off, he sends a threatening look toward the entire family who cower in terror in the kitchen. Written on his face are a threat and a promise—to repeat his monsoon pilgrimage in the future. Even bubbly Subashini, always buoyant and chirpy, is dispirited toward the end of Hunger Man's visit. She has no wisecracks to offer as seeds of badly needed sunshine in Thoma's household.

Monsoon Man howls like a madman. He then crosses the front yard, abandoning his trademark black robe. He sheds it in front of the rental. He is immediately clad in a white robe. He crosses the street, paying no attention to the assembled neighbors who gawk at him.

Then, while the crowd is standing there absorbed in watching him with disbelieving eyes, he sheds his monsoon head. He becomes a one-headed giant—the harvest giant. People cheer.

He is then swept away by the last storm of the monsoon. He is gone. Thoma and family step out of home with a big sigh of relief.

"Look! There is something in the sky," Subashini says. They all look up. There is a message in the sky, inscribed in gigantic black smoke.

"See you next monsoon, my friend!" says the smoke signal.

THREE

THE LAND LORD

Monsoon season is upon Kerala spreading misery, hunger, and hopelessness. Ann gets up early. Her neighbor Bhavany also is up. The two women talk outside in the common covered patio. The very first task on each woman's plate is to prepare steaming cup of coffee to wake their husbands up and send them on their way to work. The next task would be to get the children ready for school.

"Never a dull day," says Bhavany with a smile and sigh. Ann nodes in agreement.

"Bhavany, bring my coffee, dear," Kumaran orders from the bed. Ann knows Thoma won't be far behind and hurries to prepare coffee.

Ann submits her shopping list to Thoma during the critical morning coffee.

"Rent is due today," Ann says as soon as Thoma takes the first sip. "Don't start with your shopping list," Thoma says. "I am still sleeping."

"If you are sleeping, I am snoring," Ann says with a cautious, controlled laughter. She is careful not to cross the red line with Thoma.

"What else is on your list?" Thoma asks, hoping to hear nothing more. "I met children's schoolteachers last week. Our children need fresh clothing and shoes."

Thoma takes a long sip. He moves to the easy chair, sits straight up, and lights up a beedi. He sends thoughtful smoke rings to the ceiling.

"My children are still wearing clothes when they go to school," Thoma says. "As long as they don't go naked, I am happy."

Thoma deboards the bus when darkness creeps in.

To home he hurries, to have a bath and dinner, and hit the sack. He is dead tired after spending the whole day laying bricks for a new school building in the nearby town.

Chettiar, the landlord, meets him.

"I bet you know why I'm here," Chettiar says. "Rent is due, remember?"

The landlord makes it a habit to run into Thoma on paydays to collect rent. Ann code-named the practice "tenant stalking."

"I've starving children," Thoma says and keeps walking. "They need food and clothes."

"And shoes too," he says as an after-thought.

Chettiar is a smaller man than Thoma. The tenant can make instant obituary of the landlord. However, if there is another man in Mannuthy who could match Thoma's brash self-assuredness, it is Chettiar.

Such encounters take place every month. The recurrence of the meeting and its predictable outcome becomes a foregone conclusion. Thoma's fellow passengers who de-board the bus with him are used to witnessing the never-ending saga of Chettiar demanding the rent and Thoma offering excuses. Is Thoma wishing away his responsibilities? They wonder. Or is he a decent family man struggling to make ends meet?

On one occasion, Chettiar doesn't come alone. He has two muscular thugs with him who could drill holes with just their stares. Each has donned a red handkerchief over the head, tied down with a red bandana. They belong to a group nicknamed *Rotten Mangoes,* Chettiar's rent-collection outfit consisting of muscular men and women. It is an appropriate name for a rock band, *Rotten Mangoes,* except they are anything but. They employ rotten tactics like humiliation and assault to intimidate delinquent tenants.

Thug One, so named by Thoma in his mind, unwinds his bandana and tosses his red scarf, unmasking a rock-hard, sweat-smeared skull. In the blink of an eye, he wraps the bandana around Thoma's neck, easily fending off efforts to block him. As the red cloth tightens around the neck, Thoma gasps.

"Leave me alone, you no-good son of a bitch." Thoma garbles out the trailing words as the grip tightens, making him less articulate.

"This is just an appetizer, brother!" Thug One says. "I'll serve you the main dish shortly—after my friend is done with you."

He steps aside, releasing the neck hold. A malicious-looking partner waiting in the wings, appears—Thug Two. The left side of his face has a deep scar, the result of a past knife fight. He growls.

"I bet you can't fight me man-to-man, one-on-one," Thoma says to the intimidating presence before him.

Instead of answering, he pushes Thoma toward the parked bus, and stands him with his back against it. Thoma throws punches—to no avail. The man stretches out Thoma's arms sideways and ties them onto the bus metal bar with a nylon rope he dishes out of the pocket. Thoma now looks like crucified Jesus, except blood isn't flowing—not yet.

By now a large crowd gathers around the bus—the de-boarded passengers and men and women from the adjacent shopping village.

The bus driver doesn't like someone tied to his bus; he must move on. "Untie the man; I need to leave," he shouts and jumps out of the driver's seat, moving toward the bully working on Thoma. Thug Two stops him and ties him to the bus.

"Who else wants to help Thoma? I dare you to step forward." His eyes scan the crowd, challenging anyone to join the crucified duo to make up the legendary trio of the Crucifixion—Thoma, the Jesus; bus driver on his right, Dismas the penitent thief, and the third on the left, Gestas the impenitent thief. "Where is my Gestas?" Thug Two shouts. No volunteers.

Chettiar appears on the scene. He parks a smirk on one side of his face and displays ominous mien on the other, looking like a two-face. He holds up his clenched fist; Thoma expects a blow to land on him, and readies to take one. Instead, Chettiar rubs his unshaven face with the fist, and sends a well-directed puff of beedi smoke toward Thoma. "You brought this on yourself, my friend," he says. Thoma's knee jams into Chettiar's balls; the landlord buckles and sits in slow motion.

"Way to go, Thoma," the crowd cheer.

Thug One draws a knife and brandishes it in front of Thoma. The frightened crowd scrambles to see a murder; they implore him to be lenient. "Forgive Thoma! Don't kill him," they scream en masse. In a quick swing, the thug tears the bandana tying Thoma's arm. In a second swing, he cuts the rope on the other arm. Thoma is free; the crowd lets out gasps of surprised relief.

"We have change of plan, you weasel," he says to Thoma. "You're to go to the bus roof so that a larger crowd can see the show."

"What show?" the crowd ask.

"The beating show; six beatings for six months of unpaid rent. Ha." One thug wraps rope around Thoma's chest while the other restrain him. The rope goes around the chest and under the armpits. The arms are tied behind. One climbs up the ladder at the bus rear and positions himself on the roof. He reaches down and pulls on the rope upward, hoisting Thoma and keeping him suspended in the air while his partner ropes his legs together. The roof thug pulls Thoma up to the bus top and stations him there.

Meanwhile Chettiar recovers from the ball-smashing kick. He ascends the ladder and joins the two men on the roof. He has with him a hockey stick with a fishnet securely tied to the end. The ground thug tosses a tennis ball to him. He expertly catches it and deposits inside the net.

"Any last words before the beating begins?" he asks Thoma, getting no reply.

The landlord stays at arm's length from the tenant and swings the hockey stick at him, whipping his head with the tennis ball. It hits Thoma like thunder. Lightning flashes in his eyes. He staggers, but Roof thug steadies him.

"One," Chettiar announces.

The ground thug now sports a loudspeaker. "One," he hollers. "One," *Rotten Mangoes* repeat. The team of young men and women are seated before the loudspeaker thug who is now pacing back and forth, holding the bullhorn.

The theatrical relay of "one" from Chettiar to the ground thug to *Rotten Mangoes* captures widespread attention. Word gets around that Chettiar's assault machine is in operation. A larger crowd gathers to attend the dramatic proceedings.

A second ball arrives flying from the ground. The net sports two balls now.

Chettiar delivers a second blow. "Two," he shouts. "Two," says the loudspeaker.

"Two," say *Rotten Mangoes*. Thoma totters but doesn't fall.

"You get two for one; lucky bastard," Chettiar says to Thoma, pointing to the two balls administering double blow in one lash.

A third ball flies. Thoma would be getting three for one, better than two for one. Chettiar reminds Thoma is getting luckier by minute.

"Three," Chettiar announces.

"Three," says the loudspeaker.

"Three," chants the choir of *Rotten Mangoes*, like a symphony orchestra performing under the direction of their conductor, the loudspeaker thug.

"Someone go get the police; where are they when we need them?" someone in the crowd shouts. "Stop the torture, you bastards!"

But then it is too late to stop the show that has already drawn considerable crowd. That was Chettiar's intent – to humiliate the tenants in front of a huge crowd. As far as he is concerned, the more the crowd, the higher the climax.

"Four," calls out Chettiar. "Two more remaining." "Four," says the loudspeaker.

"Fou—"*Rotten Mangoes* doesn't complete. There is a commotion; a fresh crowd gathers around the loudspeaker thug and *Rotten Mangoes*. There is a stampede amid pushing, shoving, shouting, and screaming.

"Stop your beating," someone says. "Leave Thoma alone!"

Thoma gazes at the riot scene and recognizes Kumaran who is leading the riot. He and his accomplices are staging an attack on Chettiar's thug group. Ann and his three children have joined the crowd.

"Don't hurt my poor husband," Ann pleads to Chettiar, wailing miserably. "He needs to go to work to bring us food." She weeps along with the children.

Kumaran climbs up the ladder. Inspired by his brave act, others join him. They wrestle with the thug and Chettiar, while others keep the *Rotten Mangoes* at bay, and Thoma out of harm's way. Kumaran unties Thoma and sets him free.

Chettiar's plan to complete a cycle of six lashes for the delinquent six months is foiled. "Six blows for six months' unpaid rent!" is what he had planned to announce at the end of the beating session, to teach his tenant an unforgettable lesson.

It is not that Thoma doesn't want to pay the rent. In his heart of hearts, he planned to do so. However, the needs of his children take precedence and foil his plan. The landlord reaches the limits of his patience and decides to take the law into his own hands, being a vigilante of sorts.

The crowd unties the bus driver.

"Everyone, get off the bus," the freed driver says. "I'm taking Thoma straight to the hospital."

In the interest of saving time, he keeps Thoma on the roof. The crowd who climbed up stay there, keeping guard on Thoma while bus is in motion to the emergency ward. Ann and children join the roof crowd.

Thoma lost two upper front teeth in the encounter. The loss is a lasting memorial to the tragic falling-out with Chettiar. Everyone gets used to his gap-toothed smile and funny way of pronouncing Malayalam words. His children imitate the new pronunciation in a skit they present at the Mannuthy Government School's festival. There is nonstop laughter.

"Your father has fewer teeth now, but he has more bones; so, we are even," Ann says to her children in a rare display of humor. The children laugh uncontrollably upon hearing the unexpected joke from their mother. They repeat it to their friends at school, who laugh even more. God, in his infinite wisdom, didn't forget to endow Ann's brain with a sense of humor, if only to put up with tough realities she faced after marrying Thoma.

Even though Thoma is assaulted and humiliated publicly, he continues to live in Chettiar's rental because he has nowhere else to go. However, he doesn't forget the beating he took.

He remembered.

"Ann's tummy is full." Subashini broadcasts the pregnancy like a news bulletin while sitting serenely in her cage and mending her feathers.

Ann keeps on giving birth after the family's arrival in Mannuthy, giving no break to her exhausted uterus, delivering babies faster than a stork flying at supersonic speed. Thoma's rental gets crowded. There are six children now, three of whom – George, Rita, and Kareena – accompanied Thoma and Ann from their ancestral home. The additions are Josh, Rafeena, and Wilma.

"Your troop is swelling," Kumaran says to Thoma. "Soon they will become men and women, and you'll have a large army under your command." Kumaran is doing the usual—giving free haircuts to Thoma and his children. The free service is on the rise year after year, thanks to Ann's hyperactive uterus.

"At this rate, you'll be supreme commander of the Indian Army." Kumaran uses a broad brush to spread the shaving cream on Thoma's facial stubble before meticulously cleaning it off with a sharp razor with a long handle.

"I offer them free to the Indian army," Thoma says, dreaming the government would take them off his hands. He would have offered them free to anyone who asked. "They are yours for the asking," Thoma says to his drinking buddies. Nobody takes up the offer.

The increased number of children gives rise to the interesting phenomenon of a shrinking house. Thoma schemes to resolve the issue. He is certain that if push comes to shove, he would take possession of the attic. He plans to annex the attic, overriding the embargo imposed by the landlord not to enter the attic.

Thoma enters the attic. He is seeing it for the first time and is surprised to learn how large it is. *Attic* is certainly a misnomer; its size qualifies it to be called a regular-sized living quarter. Thoma and his children retrieve Chettiar's belongings. There are bloodstained statues of the goddess Kali—a Hindu goddess of death. Littered all over the attic floor are abandoned toddy bottles. There are tools used to perform black magic. The attic walls were strewn with bewildering scratch marks. It is as if a wolf was let loose to scrape to its heart's content. Thoma and his elder children collect the items and haul them downstairs. They clean out the attic and move their belongings there.

"Kids, are you on your best behavior?" Chettiar calls out as he heads toward Thoma's rental to inspect the premises. Thoma knows that he is in big surprise if he could see what was done to the forbidden zone, the attic..

The first item that hits Chettiar is goddess Kali's bronze statue. He sees stars when Kali kisses his forehead.

"You bastard, What do you think you—" He can't complete the sentence, because Thoma throws a toddy bottle landing smack in the middle of the forehead.

"I'll show you beggars who the boss is around here," Chettiar says after getting up from where he was felled by a plank of wood Thoma launched at him.

Chettiar's able-bodied sons Ravi and Sasi appear.

"I dare you to fight with us, you slimeball," Thoma rolls up his shirt sleeves. Thoma's children fling a barrage of rocks.

The men and children throw themselves at one another. Muscular Thoma easily outmaneuvers the landlord; he lifts Chettiar and holds him above his head as if in a weight-training class. His left hand holds Chettiar's neck in a viselike grip, and his right hand grips his feet. He spins, gathering speed and release him.

Chettiar takes off with a surprised scream. He lands across the street in the neighbor's yard. The guard dog looks at the uninvited arrival unkindly. He gnashes his teeth, growls, and vaults on the intruder. His mouth locks onto the thigh.

Meanwhile, Ravi and Sasi are beating George left and right. Rita and Kareena watch the losing battle and wish they were boys for once. Kareena gets hold of a water gun she was given as a Christmas present, and squirts water at Chettiar's sons.

"Stop squirting, you little bitch," Ravi says.

"Get lost, you little dick," Kareena says She doesn't have the foggiest idea what *little dick* means. She spurts out the words to the astonishment of the gathering crowd. She has been groomed to be an expletives expert by none other than her father—Tmoma, the great master of profanity.

"Come and rescue George," Rita pleads to her father.

Thoma joins George. He tackles Ravi, leaving the other one, Sasi, to be tackled by George. Kareena, by now, graduates from water squirting to firewood throwing. With her backup, George defeats Sasi handily.

Thoma lifts Ravi and hoists him above his head. He does a Hula-Hoop motion and, with a precision only he could muster, releases Ravi, sending him exactly where he sent the landlord. The son makes violent impact with the dog, sandwiching it between him and his dad—making the dog a hot dog of sorts.

The dog is squished and howls in protest. He wiggles out from between the man and the boy and studies the second intruder with hostile eyes. Snarling, he delivers the younger visitor a gripping welcome—by biting off flesh from his biceps.

The dog eventually releases Chettiar and Ravi. Its repeated biting result in gaping gashes in Chettiar's thighs and son's biceps. The somewhat thigh-less Chettiar leaves the scene with his son, leaving a blood trail behind them.

The gaping hole in Ravi's bicep uncovers his humerus. "Oh, poor baby, did the dog tickle your funny bone?" Kareena asks with a chuckle. She learned about the humerus, or funny bone, in her fifth-grade anatomy class.

Thoma and his family celebrate their victory. It is a rare moment of happiness that cuts through the darkness of the night. They finish moving the left-over belongings into the attic. Being spring-loaded, the attic door closes automatically when released. Thoma didn't lock the door; he didn't need to. The attic is freely accessible to the family.

"This is against the rental contract," shouts Chettiar to his lawyer about Thoma's attic annexation. Thoma and Ann are present.

"Where is the signed lease agreement?" the lawyer asks.

"Sir, I burned it to fuel my oven," Ann says. "I ran out of the wood fuel."

The lawyer accuses Thoma of illegal occupancy. The case filed never reaches a court of law, but it makes the lawyer very rich; nothing else happens. Ann considers it a sign from God. She is convinced the Mannuthy rental is their permanent abode. "We are like the people of Israel who reached the Promised Land; this Mannuthy rental is our own Promised Land, our ultimate salvation," she says to Thoma and children.

Thoma installs a palm-leaf curtain on the front porch. The curtain comes up at night and comes down in the morning. The neighborhood children gaze at the newly hung curtain curiously. They say Thoma's family is staging a nightly play.

"What is the name of the play?" Ravi askes. "*Thoma's Curtain,*" says Sasi.

"Who are the actors?"

"Thoma and Ann. The drama club doesn't sell tickets to the public; it is a family show, open only to the actors."

"A play without audience? Hmm... Never heard of it."

The play commences when Thoma and Ann retreat into kitchen when the curtain drops at night and children fall asleep. It continues until dawn when the curtain is drawn. This contrasts with the conventional play which commences when the curtains are drawn and concludes when dropped.

Thoma's Curtain is a family drama, Thoma and Ann are main actors; children have only sleeping roles. The clay oven and pots in the kitchen and a cross hanging on the dark kitchen wall bear witness to their passionate lovemaking. The actors scare away the lizards and rats in the kitchen. The neighbor's dog which materializes in the kitchen through a hole in the door barks loudly in protest and leave. Subashini sits in the cage hanging from the kitchen ceiling, closes her eyes, pretends to see, and hear nothing, and decides to say nothing of the nightly play.

Ann is the undisputed queen of the kitchen and feels quite at home there—it is her most favorite room where she is accustomed to cooking with a wood-burning stove called clay oven. She crouches on the floor and blows into it ad infinitum, with her face darkening like cinder as time goes by. She loves making love in a warm kitchen. While the lovemaking is going on, Rita and Kareena are sound asleep in the interior bedroom and George in the outside porch, blissfully unaware that father and mother are having nightly rendezvous behind their backs.

The girls thought Ann always slept with them and George thought the same—that Thoma slept with him.

"Since mom and dad sleep separately, do they plan not to make babies?" Kareena, the third grader, asks Rita, the fourth grader.

"The stork brings the babies," Rita says. "That is what mom says." "That is not true!" Kareena says. "Isha tells me that babies are born when father and mother sleep together." Isha is her classmate.

This is surprising news to Rita. The girls confront Ann. "The stork brings babies. However, they become alive only when Mom and Dad sleep together," Ann says after a quick thinking.

The girls are delighted to get updates on the baby factory.

The raw sounds and moans of lovemaking wakes up the rooster sleeping on one leg in the backyard. He cries out, "Cock-a-doodle-doo."

This wakes up Bhavany, the neighbor. She moves the hairy arms of Kumaran off her bare breasts without interrupting his snoring. She collects her opulent black hair that is tossed around, partly eclipsing Kumaran's face. She sits up on the bed, listens to the rooster once more, and makes up her mind that the morning has broken. She gets out of the bed to go to the nearby temple for the Morning Prayer. Recently she has been praying for a second child. She puts on a white cotton sari, applies red bindi on her forehead, and adorns her hair with fresh jasmines.

When she opens the front door on the way out, the creaking sound alerts Kumaran who immediately gets up and restrains Bhavany. "Come back to bed, hon," he says. "It is still night. The goddess can wait until morning."

The exhilarating fragrance of Jasmine gracing Bhavany's hair makes him drunk with passion, and she gives birth to their second daughter nine months later.

Years later, Bhavany would tell her second daughter that she was born when Thoma and Ann made love in the neighboring kitchen.

Ann chews on a betel leaf spiced with white lime paste and areca nuts.

She chews on this mix as tirelessly as cows chew on grass and spits out its red saliva. Chickens and ducks assemble around the spit to gossip about Thoma's family. Her spit is their water cooler.

She is worried Thoma is into heavy drinking. As for Thoma, toddy is elixir of immortality, uplifting his moods and breathing life into his existence.

"Toddy is my real wife, and I go to bed with her," Thoma brags to his drinking buddies in the nearby toddy club. "She is my first wife; I married her before I married Ann," he lights up a beedi and sings funny songs.

Alcohol brings out his inner singer. Most nights he sleeps with a toddy bottle by his side, happily feeling he is sleeping with his girlfriend, his mistress, his real wife.

Ann is aware, as Subashini can attest, that he often beats her with his powerful, swinging arms under the pretext of beating a mosquito off her. He blames Ann for everything bad in the world, including flies, mosquitoes, and moths, and concludes she deserves a beating occasionally, to set things right. This gets worse on the days he gets drunk on toddy. "Thoma, don't get drunk; you'll see mosquitos," Ann says. On drunken nights, he seems to see more mosquitos. Subashini would be awake on some such occasions and would see the beating coming. "Look out! Thoma hit," she squawks. Ann moves fast, narrowly escaping the assault.

She is often a sitting duck, excruciatingly slow in her motion. The town's gossip mill goes into overdrive with an unusual story of her birth. God creates a statue from clay, intending to breathe life into it to create Ann, the standard practice in making a human. But something unusual happens in the process. The statue starts moving with halting steps even before God breathes life into it. He releases her to earth as a slow-moving phenomenon.

Her kitchenware including crumbly clay pots hanging on the kitchen wall watches her cooking as if done in a slow-motion movie. She realizes that speed is essential to dodge Thoma's arm swings meant to beat the daylights out of her.

"Attend self-defense class," Bhavany advises her. "It's the only way to escape Thoma's beating."

"Beating is his way of showing masculinity," Ann says.

"Thank God Mannuthy doesn't have many masculine men," Bhavany says. "Otherwise, many Mannuthy housewives will have no limbs."

"One for the road." Thoma places order at Mannuthy's toddy shop. "Don't drop it and break it," the man at the counter tells him. He looks at Thoma with concern and adds, "Don't trip over the roadside bushes or run into a bullock cart, my friend."

At home he drinks the packaged toddy. Ann and children don't dare approach him while he drinks. When he snores, they pry loose the bottle out of his grip, praying to Mother Mary for their safety through-out the delicate operation—it is like they are near a sleeping lion in its den. They drain out toddy and replace it with starch water that Ann extracted from boiled rice.

Toddy is of the same white color as starch water but not as viscous. A drunken Thoma can't tell the difference, so the family figures.

"This toddy isn't good like it used to be," Thoma declares to the bedroom walls later when he takes a sip between his sleeps. The family struggles to suppress their laughter but fail. Their laughter rings out loud in the silence of the night.

One day, Thoma's drinking buddies carry him home. This is unusual; Ann is accustomed to seeing him coming home singing and dancing and knocking at the wrong house—Bhavany's. She steers him to Ann; that is how a normal day ends. But today is different; he loses his balance and bumps into a bullock cart which tramples him; his buddies do Good Samaritan's job of carrying him home. They leave him on the porch and throw away his take-out toddy bottle—nicknamed *one for the road* by Ann and the children.

"He had one too many for the night," they say and leave.

Thoma eventually gets up. Ann had cooked fish curry and boiled rice.

After chewing a blob of rice dipped in fish gravy, he stands up.

"Rice is overcooked," he roars. "Make it evenly cooked." His clay plate is airborne. It makes hard landing, disintegrating, and spraying the rice all over. The children look at the madman with fear, expecting a blow to land on Ann any moment.

"You want me to do miracles, Thoma?" Ann says. "Show me how to take away the cooking part from the overcooked rice." The children chuckle nervously.

"Here's the miracle you need." He pulls her to him and delivers a sucker punch.

Bhavany, the good neighbor, would hear about Ann's comment the very next day and have a hearty laugh. "Ann was right," she says to Kumaran. "Cooking rice is an irreversible process; you can't take out the cooking part from cooked rice. Every housewife knows it."

"Then don't overcook the rice." Kumaran defends Thoma, another househusband.

Thoma follows up his sucker punch with a barrage of blows, both forehand and backhand, like in tennis, on the undefended one-woman army of Ann. She moves backward to duck the blows, but Thoma keeps up, moving forward in synchrony with her backward march. The forehand blow tilts her face to the right, and the backhand to the left. These rapid-fire blows make her perfectly imitate an owl, turning left and right in quick succession.

She reaches the end of the room and is up against the wall, both literally and figuratively. She turns around and resumes her backward march, being too focused on blow absorption, and disoriented like a deer caught in headlights, to run away from him. Thoma follows her, coordinating his movement with hers like a synchronized swimmer. Soon the opposite wall blocks her, and the process repeats.

"I'll make fresh rice for you; stop beating me," Ann says. Thoma seems not to hear. He keeps on beating like a festival drum beater too excited to stop.

The three children look on helplessly. The very first sobbing came from George, then the others. They cry in unison, staging an un-orchestrated symphony of loud weeping.

"Mom, block the blows with your hand," Kareena says from the sidelines. She and Rita send their representative, George to the battlefield to defend their mother. George approaches Thoma and timidly pulls his father's *mundu* to get him away from Ann and disrupt the beating cycle.

Mundu falls off, leaving Thoma in shorts. Thoma turns around and pushes George so hard that he travels faster than light, violating the law of Relativity. George topples the dining table, along with the overcooked rice.

He picks himself up and stands there as if in a daze, but the younger siblings push him back to the battle zone.

"Get moving, George, for the love of God," Rita says.

George expertly places himself between Thoma's invading army and Ann's retreating army. This interception enrages Thoma. He switches gears and starts delivering freshly minted blows to George. Soon, George, in a perfect imitation of Ann, tilts his head left and right and walks backward like a receding owl.

George's intervention allows Ann to take a badly needed break. Rita and Kareena surround her and massage her face with their little hands, consoling her and crying at the same time. Ann starts preparing fresh rice, giving instructions to the girls to make sure it won't be overcooked.

The mother can't stomach her eldest son being beaten by a maniacal father. She reenters the battlefield and interposes herself between Thoma and George. Once more, Thoma switches gears, abandons George, and resumes beating Ann.

George gets away and rubs blows off his face. He then collects his sisters to fend off the artillery fire from the patriarch. The children's army steps forward. George holds on to Thoma's shorts for dear life, and the sisters throw themselves at their dad's feet, letting Ann get away.

Thoma's beating spree continues after Ann is rescued. He is unaware that Ann left—he had been too drunk. He keeps on marching and beating the imaginary Ann that he keeps seeing in front of him. He progressively moves forward, turning back around at the wall and beating the daylights out of thin air.

He is reduced to beating invisible mosquitoes.

FOUR

HORROR IN ANN'S KITCHEN

"My children are the accidental tourists who dropped by during my love festival with you," Thoma declares when he gets up. Ann was up earlier to prepare the morning coffee. She joins him with a steaming cup carefully held in her right hand. He moves to the easy chair and sits straight up.

"Did you get some revelation during the night's sleep?" Ann asks with a mocking face and hands over the coffee. "Or is this the Word according to Prophet Thoma?"

Thoma takes the first sip of the day. He carefully places the cup on the edge of the bed and lights up a beedi and sends smoke rings up into the ceiling.

"Keep the children with you as long as you like. I want no role in their upbringing."

"They're your own children," Ann says. "Treasure them like jewels." "Hang them on your ears if they are jewels."

"One day you'll know they are the treasures of your life. They're our gifts from God; treasure them and love them, Thoma!"

"Your children will amount to nothing. Mark my words." Thoma qualifies the children as *your children* to Ann.

"You don't mean that, Thoma! I know you don't. You love your children, but you are afraid to show it. Be bold. Loving is not beneath you; it makes you stronger."

Ann suspects that Thoma, despite his bravado, is a weak man inside. His macho mannerism is a facade concealing his troubling flaws in courage.

"Why are you afraid of showing love? Love's display doesn't emasculate you. The children love you. Return that love. They are children today but adults tomorrow. It'll be too late to show your love when they are adults."

Thoma opens the window and spits sharply into the yard. Ann knows that is the end of the morning conversation.

The rain batters the grounds. The day looks dark because of the collected clouds yet to rain down. The chickens and ducks take asylum on the veranda. They stand frozen like statues, staring at the raindrops cascading down from the sky.

Ann is in the kitchen mid-morning, wondering when the rain would end. She sports long curly hair tied down in a single knot. It hangs like Rapunzel's hair. She is wearing freshly ironed chatta and mundu. Thoma has gone to work, and the children are in the school. Bhavany is attending a wedding in her extended family. Ann remembers that she saw her neighbor carrying an outsized umbrella and boarding the bus earlier in the day.

The day's menu is fish curry and tapioca. Thoma loves it; so, do the children. She takes out the sickle and starts cutting tapioca, crouching on the floor.

Chettiar walks in, an unwelcome sight to her eyes. He is a middle-aged man, baldness claiming most of the real estate on the head. He is wearing a red mundu and is naked from the waist up. Casually tossed over his shoulder is a bath towel.

"How did you get in here?" Ann is surprised that he walked into the kitchen from the interior of the rental, because she had locked all the accesses to the kitchen earlier. Thoma insisted she did this, especially when she is alone at home. "Visitors aren't welcome when you are alone," Thoma has said often.

Chettiar doesn't answer. She isn't used to seeing him or talking to him, let alone when she is alone in the privacy of her home. There is a distant, cold relationship between the landlord and her.

The hardened lines on his face curve crookedly, sketching a mean man. His eyes are restless, and they dart in all possible directions as if to focus on something he can lay claim to, and charge rent on.

"Rent is due," Chettiar says. A quick message with no preliminary pleasantries. The delivery of the three words is abrupt and hostile. It is the first of the month, Ann realizes.

"Thoma pays the rent, not me," Ann says. "How did you get in? I had locked all the doors!"

"Let us just say I came from inside the wall," he jokes with devilish grin exposing his tobacco-stained yellow teeth. He plunks himself down on the kitchen bench. "Maybe I dropped from the sky." He looks around the kitchen that is sporadically illuminated by the monsoon lightning.

"Don't sit there like a statue. Pay the rent," he says.

Ann continues to sit. She is unable to think, caught off guard in the sanctuary of her kitchen by the unexpected arrival of a possibly dangerous man. Thunder roars. The guard dog across the street barks. Ann mobilizes her brain and ponders how to respond to him and deliver the message of no rent money without landing herself in trouble. Finally, she decides to shoot it straight. "Sorry, I don't have it."

His face becomes contorted with anger. Ann hears his teeth grinding. "Sorry doesn't cut it, you bitch! Pay up, or to hell you go." The malice on his face says he would stop at nothing to get what he is owed. His eyes turn reddish. They focus on Ann like those of a snake homing in on its prey. She feels she is about to be snared.

"When my husband gets home, I'll ask him. We'll work out something. Don't be mad. Please."

Chettiar stands up but sits down immediately, unable to keep balance. Ann senses he is drunk. He stands up again, holds on to the walls, and walks toward her. He closes the kitchen door behind him, alarming Ann.

"Keep the door open! Thoma will come anytime." She lies; she knows Thoma won't be in until after dark.

Darkness deepens as soon as the door is closed. The weak glow of the fire in the clay oven struggles to spread light. Ann can barely make out the figure of the intruder. The lightning flashes disclose his silhouette moving toward her—two glowing eyes gravitate toward her. Those eyes come close. Very close. She then realizes she was like a deer caught in the headlights— too transfixed by his presence to move away.

"Get out of my kitchen; leave our home," Ann screams. The moving eyes stop.

He pulls her Rapunzel hair and stands her up, heavily leaning on her to steady himself. Ann is disgusted by the man's touch and alcohol stench. She moves left and right in tune with his unsteady footsteps. They resemble slow dancers in a county fair's dance festival, except there is no music.

Instead, there are sounds of thunder and flashes of lightning. She tries to break loose from his grip, no success.

"You want me to get out of kitchen, do you?" he asks. "Just whose house you think this is?"

Releasing his hold on her hair, he stands back and beats her so hard that she reels and drops the sickle and the fish. The force of the beating lands her against the wall. She recoils and collapses on the floor, screaming at the top of her voice. He loses balance after delivering the blow and collapses on top of her. She wiggles from under him and gets hold of the fallen sickle and does something unimaginable : she swings the sickle at the fallen man. It strikes him in the forehead. He lets out a scream. She runs out from the kitchen.

"I'll get you, bitch!" He chases her and drags her back to the kitchen.

The lightning strikes and its flash lasts for a long time. It is as if Mother Nature wanted to witness the horror show in Ann's kitchen in its disquieting vividness. In that long-lasting flash, Ann shudders to find that Chettiar had stripped off his clothes. A brief moment of darkness follows and then another long flash. What she sees during the second flash is something out of this world. Long hair sprouts all over his body. He growls like a werewolf at the lightning, as if the brilliant flash reminded him of a full moon. A werewolf?

Ann takes advantage of the split second his attention is riveted by the lightning. She runs out the door when a blow lands on the back of her head. He gets hold of her hair, drags her back to the kitchen, turns her around, stands her up, and delivers a punch. The blow is so hard that she blacks out. The sickle flies from her hand. She doesn't get up from where she falls.

When she regains consciousness, she is alone, lying on the kitchen floor. The rain has stopped, sun is out, and the kitchen is brightly lit. Her legs are spread apart. She has been stripped off her chatta and mundu. The blood-stained clothes are tossed on the floor. They were ripped so badly that she can't re-use them. She wraps herself in a bath towel until she retrieves a new set of clothes.

She is filled with disgust and humiliation. Female dignity is of paramount importance, and she fears she would become disgrace to the family and would be blamed for the rape.

She decides to keep it a secret; however, she is afraid someone would find out, especially Thoma. He is God's most dangerous creation and would stop at nothing to seek revenge. There would be a funeral in Chettiar's home if Thoma so much as even suspects what happened.

She realizes something bizarre when she comes to her senses. She discovers that both the doors to the rental are locked from inside, just as they were prior to Chettiar showing up. She panics thinking he is hiding somewhere inside. She once more checks all the rooms, only to find to her relief that the madman was no more inside. How in the first place did he appear inside her kitchen?

She leaves these thoughts behind and takes a quick bath, dresses in fresh clothes, and finishes cooking before Thoma, and children would arrive.

There was someone watching the horrific rape scene—someone other than God. It was Subashini. She was in the cage that hung from the kitchen ceiling. The bird tried to fly out but to no avail. She squawked loudly hoping to attract outside attention. But the only response came from the neighbor's dog who barked and barked.

When the family arrives, Subashini broadcasts: "Ann attacks Chettiar," reversing the subject and the object of the sentence, displaying bad grammar. Thoma and children are puzzled that a saintly woman could attack anyone and takes the bird's talk as an instance of temporary insanity. Subashini has a fair share of inconsistent behaviors in the past.

Thoma finds out what happened.

He makes the discovery the same day when he and Ann retreat to kitchen behind the backs of the sleeping children. Ann shuns love-making that night, but Thoma persists, and she succumbs. She jumps in pain when he touches her. His curiosity arises, and he checks her out. To his horror, he sees bruises all over, which are concealed by chatta and mundu.

"Who did this to you?" Thoma screams. She tells him.

Thoma, the most dangerous man in Mannuthy, bolts upright, bellows like an elephant, roars like a lion, and grabs the kitchen knife.

"You bloody son of a bitch, I'll kill you." He points the toward Chettiar's house. Ann dresses quickly. "For the love of Christ, don't kill him!" Ann holds Thoma tightly, refusing to let go. Thoma pushes her out of his way, kicks the kitchen door open, and gets out to the backyard. He hurries toward Chettiar's home cursing and screaming. The children and neighbors wake up, alerted by the loud commotion. Kumaran and Bhavany come out running and see Thoma in his shorts, wielding a kitchen knife, and heading to Chettiar's home with Ann in hot pursuit.

"Today I am going to cut you up like fish," Thoma says, gazing at Chettiar's home. His booming voice thunders, and he raises his knife.

"Kumaran, please block him," Ann pleads. "Stop him before he murders Chettiar!"

By this time, all the children are out, and they surround their father.

With help from Bhavany and all the assembled children, Kumaran restrain Thoma, disarming him by tossing the knife away. He carries Thoma and place him on the bed.

Bhavany has been working as a nursing assistant at the time in the nearby medical dispensary. She has some medical supplies at home. She gives Thoma a tranquilizer shot. He is knocked out.

A disaster is prevented.

Thoma gets up early next morning. He feels very strange. He thinks he had a bad dream. On second thought, he realizes it wasn't a dream at all.

"Let us get even with Chettiar," Subashini says. They are the only two awake at that time.

"What do you have in mind?" Thoma asks.

She tells him. Thoma lets the bird out of her cage per plan.

Subashini flies out, goes two houses down the road, and settles on the ceiling fan in Chettiar's front porch. She dives down, pecks on the door, and settles back on the fan. To someone inside, it is as if someone is knocking at the door.

Chettiar's wife wakes up, alerted by the repeated knocking.

"Hey, you," she says to her sleeping husband. "Check who is at the door."

Chettiar rubs sleep off his eyes, steps out of the bed, walks to the door, and opens it, only to see no one. He gets out to investigate. Still no one. "Those damn kids!" he curses under his breath. Unruly kids on previous occasions knocked at his door only to disappear when he came out, playing tricks on him. He heads back to bed, muttering and cursing.

Subashini has been watching from the ceiling. She is ready.

She flies down like a rocket and pecks at his left eye, braving the arm swings he directs at her. She ducks his blows, dances around his attacking arms, and doggedly goes after him. He shields his eye with his hands, but it is no use. She jabs at his eye relentlessly. She loses a few feathers, but she won't get her feathers ruffled under any circumstance.

"Next time, you'll lose the other eye," she says and flies back to Ann's kitchen. She made sure not to take out both the eyes per Thoma's instruction during their planning session. "I need him to see me after your attack, so leave one eye untouched." He'd told her.

Thoma walks down to Chettiar's house. The neighborhood is peaceful. Everyone is still asleep. Chettiar is on his porch, doubled over and still in shock over losing his eye; He is crouched on the floor—not unlike Ann on the previous day's attack, Thoma thinks. The very first kick makes the landlord fly. He lands against the wall and collapses. He looks around to see what hit him; He spots Thoma with his right eye.

He knows that Thoma knows.

The commotion makes Chettiar's wife come out to investigate. As soon as she sees the dangerous-looking Thoma on her porch with a sickle, she screams and escapes into the house.

Because the landlord's left hand is busy massaging his left eye socket, Thoma holds an advantage over him. It is his two arms against the landlord's one fighting arm—not that Thoma needed any advantage over him. Thoma throws yuca roots and a sickle to the floor. "Cut them up to make our curry. Ann is not cooking today," Thoma informs.

When Chettiar completes the cutting, Thoma sucker-punches him so hard that he flies to the wall, ricochets, and collapses.

"Is this how you beat up my wife yesterday?" Thoma says and collects the cut-up pieces and heads back home. After couple of steps, he turns back.

"You're nothing but scum," Thoma says—more to the world than to Chettiar.

In nine months, Jaygust is born.

Ann feels that the story of his birth is too horrid, stopping people in their tracks when they hear it and making them abandon faith in the goodness of human nature.

As the pregnancy advances into the third trimester, it becomes apparent that she is carrying the elephant god's son because her womb becomes abnormally large. Her tummy bulges out and gyrate, taking up quite a space in front of her. She struggles to manage her abnormal pregnancy, her sagging belly hampering her attempts to sit, lie down, or stand.

"You have ten jackfruits in your belly," Bhavany says. The good neighbor often visits Ann during her grueling pregnancy.

Ann gives birth to twins, a boy, and a girl. The girl looks just like Ann, and the boy like Chettiar. Ann watches the little babies with disgust, knowing well whose babies they are. The whole of Mannuthy knows; it is an open secret.

A few months after the delivery, Ann is asleep while the babies are huddled over her bare breasts. The boy is drinking from her right breast, and the girl from the left. The girl gravitates to the right breast because she wasn't getting enough from the left. She nudges the boy away from the right breast and sucks on it. As soon as the territorial fight advances to the girl's advantage, baby boy's screaming wakes Ann up.

She is surprised to see him standing, since he is not yet of the age when he could do so. And then she sees something extraordinary: he is covered in long body hair, like a baby wolf! With his tiny body covered in hair, he looks like a fur ball.

The boy fixes a malicious scowl on his face as only an adult could. He then wraps his little hands around the girl's neck and lifts her up, standing there like a mini-Samson and strangling his sister with super-human strength. The little girl stops drinking, gasps, and lets out a muf-fled scream.

Ann manages to roll out of the bed and start pulling out the girl but can't shake off the boy's grip. Her hands slip, throwing her backward. She trips on the bassinet resting on the floor, loses balance, and does a backward somersault, landing against the wall and falling. When she picks herself up and approaches the bed, the inevitable has happened. The baby girl is not moaning any more. The boy has strangled her.

Ann sees another extraordinary thing. Right in front of her eyes, the boy starts losing his body hair, and he becomes his normal self. He falls asleep on the bed. She gazes at the sleeping baby boy—sleeping like a baby after committing murder.

Ann insists on naming the boy Disgust because he is born from an act of disgust. This is such an outrageous name that the Mannuthy par-ish priest ask her to consider renaming. She eventually settles for Jaygust, an unusual name for a human being. She felt that justice is nevertheless done—the name retains the *gust* of *disgust*, and it would be a lasting reminder of the horrendous rape she'd surrendered her dignity to.

Jaygust is Ann's seventh child, but not of Thoma. The sight of Jaygust, the permanent sickle mark on Chettiar's forehead, and the man's lost left eye reminded her of the unmentionable assault that took place in her sanctum sanctorum, her kitchen.

Jaygust becomes known as Cradle Strangler.

Thoma and his boys continue to sleep on the front porch. Jaygust sleeps alone in the attic. It is a creepy room, and the rest of the children avoid it. Ann and the six girls continue to sleep in the bedroom behind the kitchen. The bedroom is directly below the attic, connected by a staircase.

The girls notice something. They sneak peeks at the sleeping boys on the porch at night. Then they start counting: one, two, and so on. No, it isn't the boys they count. The erections become prominent as time goes on.

"Thoma's children are growing up," Subashini says.

The exciting sight makes headlines. Soon it becomes a topic of intense nightly discussion among the girls: those erect penises that stand in their nightly glory like the cannons of Tipu Sultan in the Fourth Anglo-Mysore War in 1799. The boys' canons stand erect and alert, ready to fire at an angle of forty-five degrees to give maximum range to the cannonballs per the laws of physics. The girls watch the nightly phenomenon, throwing modesty to the winds.

"Our soldiers are on duty; they are standing at attention," Kareena says.

"They're our nightly guards protecting us," the girls whisper. They salute the soldiers, admire their sleepless vigilance, and go back to sleep, feeling safe, convinced that the soldiers will guard them even when their masters are negligently asleep.

"The soldiers are awake, but the bodies are sleeping" they murmur, paraphrasing the famous Bible quotation, "The spirit is willing, but the flesh is weak"[2]—from the scene where Judas betrayed Christ. Jesus was awake, but his disciples fell asleep during the night of his encounter with the high priests when he was given away by Judas, who handed his master to his enemies with a kiss on his face.

"They are upstanding soldiers; they are standing up," Rita says with a mischievous twinkle in her eyes.

"Soldiers are standing up," Subashini repeats from the cage.

The girls roar with surprised laughter at the unexpected announcement from the parrot. Subashini is a girl, after all. The always-vigilant parrot doesn't mince words to describe what she sees.

"Shut up, you little girl," Kareena says to Subashini.

"Shut up, you little girl," Subashini retorts.

The calendar pages flip; time travels in its majestic chariot. Very many monsoons arrive with thunderous downpours and leave like lambs. A few thousand sunsets over the Arabian Sea follow so many sunrises over the Western Ghats.

The year 1964 arrives.

Eleven years passed since Jaygust was born. After him, Ann gives birth to the last three of the family during 1955, 1956, and 1957. The hyperactive baby factory manufactures babies in rapid-fire sequence. The proverbial stork is kept very busy. The childbirth saga consists of nonstop episodes of pregnancies, a soap opera that Thoma and Ann coproduce. By the time they have ten children, they are saddled with unbearable burdens.

"Why did you stop at ten?" Kumaran asks Thoma during free haircuts to the family.

"It's Ann's doing," Thoma says. "How so?"

"Ann uses fingers to count," Thoma says. "She can't count beyond ten."

The children break into laughter.

"Why can't you lay eggs and sit on them?" Thoma asks Ann, being hardly able to stand her hanging around with bulging tummy. "Are you salivating at that possibility?" Ann is furious.

"Of course!" says Thoma. "Then I will have you out of my hair for a number of nine-month intervals when you sit on egg for hatching."

Ann had never thought of the possibility. "How many years will my pregnancy months add up to?" She asks Kareena who is good in Math.

Kareena scribbles on a newspaper used as fish wrapping. "Seven and a half years," the daughter says.

This answer gives Ann a jolt. Sitting on eggs would have decommissioned her for seven and a half years! She would have been out of sight of her husband and children for a long time. It is too much of a sacrifice, she says, and thanks God for giving women pregnancy instead of making them sit on eggs.

Thoma and Ann can't keep track of their children's names; there are so many. "It is your job to remember the names," Thoma says to Ann.

"Why not you?" Ann fought on rare occasions. "I didn't become pregnant all by myself!"

Number Eight is a girl named Thalli, Number Nine a boy, Noman, and—finally—Number Ten, Curly, a girl.

Thalli earns her nickname from the word *thalli*, which means *beaten*—not because she was beaten but because her father was beaten at the time she was inside Ann's tummy. Thoma is nine months behind in rent payment at a time when, coincidentally, Ann is nine months pregnant with Thalli.

The landlord and his gang beat up Thoma occasionally, since Thoma was frequently delinquent in his rent payments. Chettiar's confrontation with Thoma on those occasions has a method to its madness. The landlord's hired hands give Thoma as many blows as however many months he is behind in rent payment. Thoma ends up in the hospital's emergency ward by the end of the beating.

Just prior to Thalli's birth, Chettiar and his team confront Thoma and beat him up, delivering head blows nine times. Ann is nowhere near, but her unborn baby Thalli becomes distressed and stirs frantically in her uterus.

The baby jumps nine times as if affected by the distant beatings. This is reminiscent of a spooky phenomenon of physics known as *action at a distance,* whereby an object responds to an act happening far away. The baby feels the pain through psychic connection.

Unlike other babies who come to this world with soft moaning, Thalli produces such a high-pitched devilish shrieking that both Ann and the attending midwife scream in terror. The midwife uses forceps to extract Thalli from Ann. She then snips and ties the umbilical cord, clean the baby, and places her by Ann's side. Ann looks at the baby and is petrified to see the ugliest baby of charcoal color resting by her side—a dark duckling. The baby has eight arms spread around her and is staring at Ann. Ann thinks that the midwife brought a devil's baby from the maternity ward in hell.

The baby is the spitting image of Bhadrakali, the idol goddess of Kodungallore Temple in Central Kerala. Thalli is holding the butchered head of Chettiar in one of her eight arms—just like Bhadrakali held the head of Asura, the demigod. As the days went by, six of the baby's eight arms disappear, leaving behind a normal baby girl. Ann worries that one day Thalli will kill Chettiar and that the bizarre scene is a premonition of the disaster that lie in the future. The mother feels that her newborn baby is psychic, demonic, and dangerous.

Thalli, the embodiment of wild animal looks, has a rugged dark skin. She is unlike Ann's all other children, who are of wheatish complexion. She has long flowing black hair, which redeems her overall repulsive appearance—it throws in a much-needed humanity.

FIVE

FROM KAREENA WITH LOVE

Thoma reads Kareena's letter. "My dearest father, mother, brothers, and sisters."

He, Ann, and children assemble at night to read the first letter from Kareena. She left home to take up a job with Indian government in Rajasthan located over thousand miles from Kerala.

Thoma and Ann use the same pair of reading glasses. She wipes the glasses clean and hands it to her husband.

"My dearest father, mother, brothers, and sisters." Thoma repeats the opening line in slow motion, glaring at everyone. His dramatic act captivates the audience. Ann adjusts kerosine lamp's flame.

> *It is with untold happiness that I write to you. Writing this is like talking to you in person. My heart aches when I think of you, and I yearn to be with you at our home—yes, at our home that leaks in the rain, at our home with no food to eat in rainy season. Yet isn't it strange that while living there I wished to get out, and now, I am yearning for it?*

Kareena was born during the glorious days of Thoma's family history. Those were the days when they lived in the ancestral property at Amballore, when he was able to put food on the table. However, once they relocated to Mannuthy rental, tables were turned.

It was with pure joy that I boarded the train carrying me to Rajasthan. I can't explain the roaring wildness of sheer happiness that took over my heart when the train left the station. The anticipation of the unknown future with its many possibilities excited me. I remember that every one of you was at the railway platform with teary eyes.

Ann borrows Thoma's reading glasses and reads the sentences herself, just to be sure. She then resumes rolling the rosary beads.

Kareena sends letters regularly after she leaves. Her family savor every letter, analyzing and critiquing every word. The letter goes from hand to hand, and everyone reads it once more. It takes a week for this process to be over. At the end of the week, Ann quietly smuggles the letter to Bhavany, the good neighbor. Bhavany reads the letter as if it is from her own daughter.

Kareena takes Jaygust, her younger brother, with her so he could attend school while she is at the job. She enrolls him at a better school than the one in Mannuthy, and provides him with room and board. This is a blessed relief for Thoma since he gets two birds in the same shot.

"Two fewer plates on the dining table, plus I get monthly checks from my daughter," Thoma says to Ann. "A win-win situation."

Chettiar, the landlord, is at the platform to see off his tenants. Ann knows the mean man turned up to bid goodbye to Jaygust, his son, and not necessarily to Kareena. She averts her eyes to avoid eye contact with her rapist, who has the gall to appear at her family gathering to lay an invisible claim on his son. She shudders at seeing the landlord hugging Jaygust.

Subashini is sitting on Thoma's shoulder. She is sad. "Goodbye, Kareena, my friend and sister! Remember us when you reach heaven," The bird gathered from the family conversations that any place away from Mannuthy is heaven.

The long train departs with a deafening sound, shaking the platform as if it is seized by an earthquake. The family has teary eyes long after the train disappears and long after the train's smoke dissipates along the tracks.

I was getting farther from you with every minute on the train. My feelings were bittersweet: bitter because I was departing from Kerala and sweet because I was embarking on a dream career.

I watched the raindrops that hung in the distance from the plantain leaves, refusing to fall and yet ordained to do so. I was like those raindrops, reluctantly dropping out of my motherland to an unfamiliar landscape.

Coconut palms at arm's length from the rail track swayed in the glorious breeze; I wouldn't see them for a long time to come.

My memories of Kerala will always be linked to those trees—majestic, tall, slender, and vibrant. The train whisked me away from the feast of natural beauty that Kerala always was, always is, and always will be!

The poetic description holds the family spellbound. They love her more now than when she'd been with them. It takes distance to feel real love.

Thoma closes his eyes for several seconds before continuing with the letter.

The crimson rays of the setting sun painted the landscape. The sunset marked my closing chapter in Kerala. It was a prelude to an unknown morning in Rajasthan. I crossed Kerala's border when a full moon appeared. A multitude of glimmering stars anxiously watched me move forward. The night was not still; raindrops poured down on the speeding train, reminding me of many nights when I slept at our home drenched in the rain.

Let me conclude with a promise that I will keep on hoping as I have always done. I will keep on hoping because hope begets hope. It gives the surprising illusion of the disappearance of the darkness around me. I will keep on hoping, if only to rekindle passions doomed to inevitably fade away. Shall I say I dare to dream?

I send my love to you all. I hope one day we will be reunited in Kerala and live together happily ever after, just like in fairy tales.

From Kareena, with love.

"Surging optimism permeates her letters," Thoma says to Ann. "Though at times clouds of depressive thoughts descend into them like the dark clouds of the monsoon."

Jaygust turned seventeen in 1970. That was three years after he and Kareena arrived in Rajasthan.

She hired a private tutor to help him advance in his studies. There were great expectations that he would do well and be able to get a decent job, which would give Thoma and Ann a well-deserved break.

It is close to midnight. Kareena is in the bed sleeping. Something wakes her up. It is a sound, more like a howling. As soon as she wakes up, the howling stops. It sounded like coming from the other end of the house where Jaygust has his bedroom. The home is spacious with three bedrooms and two bathrooms. Her bedroom with attached bathroom is at one end of the flat. The other end has two bedrooms and the second bathroom. The two ends of the house are interconnected by a large kitchen, a living room, and a connecting hallway.

It is full moon. The cool moonlight filters through window blinds and bathes her bedroom in a milky glow. She slides back into sleep when the howling stops. Briefly after, the howling resumes, waking her up again. This time the sound continues well after she wakes up. She thinks a dog got inside the home and Jaygust is under attack. She puts on her nightgown but doesn't dare to get out. "Jaygust, are you OK?" she calls out.

There is no reply. Is the howling getting closer? It is! She locks the room. Pinning her ear against the closed door, she listens. She hears footsteps outside in the hallway. Who is it? Her heartbeats are audible now.

"Jaygust, answer me! Are you awake?" she calls out again, screaming loudly. No answer. As if in response to her question, the footsteps stop.

"Jaygust, wake up! There is a wolf in the house!" No response. Either he is asleep, or a wolf killed him. She is the animal's next prey, she panics.

A knock at her door!

She turns numb with fear. The knock propels her thought machine into overdrive. How can a wolf knock at her door, or any door for that matter? She is in the police force and knows a thing or two about dog training. No amount of training can make a wolf knock at a door. A crazy thought flashes through her mind: you cannot teach an old dog a new trick, but how about teaching a young dog a new trick, say, knock at a door?

Maybe it is a young wolf knocking. She is about to burst into insane laughter at the thought, but gravity of the situation pulls her back.

A loud roaring ring out in the hallway. Then another knock.

She thinks quickly. She pushes the wheeled bed and places it against the door. It must be a human who knocked at her door! The intruder has a dog that is howling. That must be it. She stands on the bed on tiptoe but is not tall enough to reach the glass partition above the door. She listens intently, cocking her ear against the door. This time, the knocking and howling happen simultaneously.

"Get out of our house. I will call the police," she says.

If it is a wolf able to knock, it should equally be able to understand spoken words, she figures.

"Jaygust, come save me!" She curses him for sleeping through the ordeal.

"I order you to speak to me; I'm a police officer," she tells the intruder. Working in the police force, she knew how to give a threatening order. If need be, she is prepared to arrest the intruder, wolf or not.

The wolf answers this time. The animal howls and thrashes its fists on the door.

"Open the door," it says in garbled voice.

A talking wolf? The voice sounded vaguely familiar, but she can't place it. She hears the animal running across the hallway. It runs away from the door, and now it is coming back with quickening steps! CRASH! It bangs so forcefully that the door starts giving in. BANG! BANG! BANG!

The door gives in.

The force of impact vaults the bed off the floor, throwing it across the room and toppling Kareena who was standing on it. She falls to the floor.

Something enters the room. The beast turns on the room light, heads to the window, looks at the full moon, and howls. Its whole body is covered in long hair.

"Get in the bed, you bitch," it says.

Kareena recognizes the voice immediately. It is Jaygust! Why is he wearing a wolf costume? Despite the crushing terror that seizes her, she studies him closely in the room light and is shocked to realize that he is not wearing a costume. Long hair has grown on him, and he looks exactly like a wolf! She is too numb with fear and surprise to be able to move.

"What the hell are you doing in my bedroom?" Kareena asks. "Get out of here!"

He lifts her with one arm, empowered by superhuman force, places her on the bed, jumps into bed, straddles her, wraps his arms around her neck, and starts strangling. The grip tightens and the howling intensifies. She was white with fear. There is, however, some remaining presence of mind in her thanks to the training sessions she had at the police force.

"Get off me, you son of a bitch." She wheezed out the words.

She spins around to prone position, momentarily releasing his hold. She spins back to lie supine and kicks Jaygust in the balls. Her strong legs toned by regular exercise on the police training grounds comes in handy.

Jaygust reels. He falls off the bed. He doubles over in excruciating pain.

"Now you know a nut sandwich is painful. Want another sandwich, bro?" She is on her feet. "Get out of my room before I call police."

She gets up early the next morning. She has made some plans during the night. While making morning coffee in the kitchen, she overhears Jaygust snoring in his bedroom. She packs all his belongings into two suitcases and arranges for a taxi to arrive in two hours.

Jaygust gets up at his regular time. When he steps into the kitchen, she is ready for him.

"This is your last day in my house. Get ready to leave. I have already packed your stuff," she says.

"Why? What happened?" he asks.

Is he surprised or does he pretend to be? He is back to his normal self as she could easily tell—he is no longer the wild animal he was at night. He no longer has the body hair he had just the previous night. He says he has no recollection of what Kareena accuses him of. He denies the nightly terror he had unleashed.

The taxi arrives. Jaygust boards it and heads out to catch the train that takes him back to Kerala.

It is two years since Kareena kicked Jaygust out of her home in 1970. At home, she relaxes listening to Carnatic music. Alone at home for the last two years, she feels safe and free. She has been keeping busy with her job, meeting the challenges of the Central Reserve Police force. Her family writes to her frequently, asking her to get married. Marriage is the last thing in her mind.

The phone rings.

"Ma'am, it is a collect call from Kerala. Will you accept the charges?" the operator piped from the other end.

The call is from Mannuthy—the very first call she receives from home. All previous contacts were through letters. She gathers that the family must have gone to a telephone exchange to place trunk call. For sure, there is some tragic news at the other end of the line. Did someone die? Thoma?

Ann?

The line hums, beeps, and snarls. Then she hears, "Kareena, is that you?" She is relieved it is Thoma, he is alive! Did Ann die? Her heart beats like drum.

"This is Kareena," she says.

She hears ear-piercing wailings in the background. She realizes that the entire family is with Thoma.

"Rafeena died last night," Thoma says.

If lightning struck her, she would not be more shocked than at the news she just received. Thoma, her brave father, is sobbing. Rafeena— the wide-eyed, beautiful Rafeena with long eyelashes and pretty smile who turned twenty-one just the previous day—died? An emblem of beauty and health, an antithesis to death and decay, died? How can it be?

"How?" she asks more to the phone than to Thoma. She asks the four walls of her flat. She asks the world, "How?"

"She went to bed after her birthday party, peaceful and happy," Thoma says. "When we got up in the morning, she was gone!" Thoma can't stop weeping.

"She was gone?"

"Gone from us, dear! She did not get up from where she slept last night. She will never ever get up. She is sleeping now like an angel."

Josh comes online with update. Rafeena was found strangled in her sleep. There were signs of a struggle, but the intruder overpowered her.

"Strangled?" Kareena asks. "Did you say she was strangled?" "Exactly."

Kareena remembers. It was two years ago when Jaygust tried to strangle her. She realizes with a shock that she would have been dead now but for her physical might that fended off his attack in her bedroom.

"What does the police say?"

"Too soon to say," Josh says. "They are still investigating."

There was an uncomfortable silence. Then Josh continues. "There is a mystery surrounding the death. Looks like there was no intruder; the bedroom's front door was not forced in. The back door at the kitchen was untouched. As you know, there is no entry to the girls' bedroom, except through these two doors." He confirms Rafeena was sleeping with the other girls and Ann in the room, as is the usual practice.

"The girl's bedroom is accessible from the attic," Kareena says. "That is true."

"Was someone sleeping in the attic?" "Jaygust."

"Then look no further."

"You may be right," Josh says without elaborating. Everyone in the family knows why Kareena kicked Jaygust out of her Rajasthan flat. Did history repeat?

Ann comes on the phone.

"Who slept inside girls' bedroom?" Kareena asks.

"Just the girls and me," Ann says. "Both the kitchen and the bedroom doors were locked from inside. Jaygust slept in the attic. The rest of the boys slept on the porch with Thoma."

Kareena figures that Josh and the rest of the family must have guessed who the killer is. They are keeping mum to protect Jaygust, the murderer.

Josh comes on the phone again. "Right now, the police are taking fingerprints from the suspected areas, including Rafeena's body," he says. "Not sure if they will identify any suspect; however, we aren't offering any help to the investigators."

"What is more important?" Kareena asks. "Punishing Rafeena's murderer or protecting him?"

"We can't take back what happened," Josh says. "However, we can prevent the situation from getting worse by not helping police. If police contact you, don't reveal Jaygust's past."

"They probably will snag him. He is known as "cradle Strangler" in Mannuthy. It is an open secret."

Kareena travels to Kerala to attend the funeral. The rental unit is in pandemonium. The investigation is going on amidst funeral preparations. Jaygust was sound asleep in the attic the whole night, per the testimony he gives. To their surprise, police can't find fingerprints around Rafeena's neck even though she was undoubtedly strangled.

"It was a professional job; the guy used gloves," the investigating officer tells his boss.

"Did she have a lover?" the boss asks.

"No, sir! She was a simple girl. No adventures. Always minded her business."

"Did you notice anything strange?" "It was a full-moon night, sir."

"So what?" his boss snarls. "What does the full moon have to do with the murder? Don't make up fairy tales."

"Very good, sir."

Kareena catches Josh when he is alone. "You are dead wrong to protect Jaygust," she says. "He should be turned in. What if he repeats it?"

"We only have circumstantial evidence," Josh says. "The only witness, Rafeena, is gone, which shuts the door close on any objective evidence."

"Don't forget Jaygust has a track record," Kareena continues. "The town by now knows that he tried to strangle me without success. They also know he strangled his twin sister to death soon after he was born. We need no more evidence."

While returning to Rajasthan after the funeral, Kareena remembers Rafeena, her younger sister, with her beautiful face adorned with flowers in the casket. The family stood around the graveyard now the casket was lowered into the pit. The priest prayed, "We commend to Almighty God our sister Rafeena, and we commit her body to the ground. Earth to earth. Ashes to ashes. Dust to dust. The Lord blesses her and keeps her. The Lord made her face to shine upon him and to be gracious unto her and to give her peace. Amen."

"Amen," Kareena murmured in the train. She wept softly.

Wilma, the sixth child of Thoma and his fourth daughter, turns twenty-one the following year, 1973. Thoma didn't have the resources to send her to college after she completed high school in 1969.

Her twenty-first birthday is attended by the entire family. Kareena arrives from Rajasthan.

"What is your birthday wish, Wilma?" Kareena asks. "To attend college!" she says excitedly.

"We hope you can do that; we pray for you."

Even though Kareena was sending regular monthly checks for the family, it was not enough to see through her university education.

Kumaran and Bhavany walk in carrying birthday cake with twenty-one candles stick brightly lit. They hug Wilma. Bhavany adjusts the birthday girl's hair and plants a marigold flower in her sumptuous hair. "May the year bring you happiness, dear," Bhavany says and kisses her cheek.

The gathered guests sing birthday songs.

"Be young and beautiful forever, Wilma!" her friends say. They shower her with hugs and kisses on their way out. The family retires for the night.

Thoma sleeps on the porch with the boys. Jaygust sleeps alone upstairs in the attic. In the bedroom underneath, the girls and Ann sleep together. Wilma is wide awake; she can't sleep, she is too excited. She dreams about college. She drifts to sleep after midnight.

The sound of footsteps wakes her up. The full moon illuminates the room, and she can spot a wolf. It is descending the staircase. She figures that the animal emerged from the attic.

But wait! Only Jaygust is upstairs; he sleeps alone there. Why is the wolf coming from there? Is her brother harmed by the animal? Probably killed? She notices that the wolf doesn't walk on all fours; it is walking upright. That sure is odd. Is she seeing things?

Dread fills her. She is too afraid to wake up Ann and sisters in case her movement would draw the animal's attention to her. She pretends to sleep by closing her eyes but monitors its movement. It pauses and peers at the sleeping girls, and resumes descending as if having made up its mind on its target.

The wolf is coming in her direction! With her heart thumping, she suppresses the scream that rises from the pit of her stomach. The animal parks by her side and lifts her up. Now she screams loud, but it is swiftly muffled by the animal; it shuts her mouth with its strong hands.

"I'll kill you if you scream." The animal talks! She faints. It carries her upstairs into the attic.

The family wakes up in the morning to the horror of Wilma having gone missing. They search the neighborhood. No one remembers her screaming if she screamed at all. The police are informed. They search far and wide, but Wilma can't be located.

The investigators wonder if she ran away. Did she voluntarily venture out in search of a happy life? Was she buoyed by the happy birthday party? Was she in search of the college she had dreamed about?

Josh's classmate Devan gets depressed after hearing the sad news. He was in love with Wilma. He attended her birthday party the previous night and brought a bouquet of twenty-one red roses to commemorate her birthday. They took a short stroll outside in the yard during the party. They walked hand in hand, looked at the stars, and basked in the milky-soft light of the full moon. She let him kiss her for the first time.

"Josh, I hope she is alive somewhere," Devan says, weeping. "She wouldn't go without telling me, will she?" I feel stupid I wished her many happy returns; there probably won't be more of them."

"Hush, Devan," Josh says. "If it is of any consolation to you, I feel very terrible myself."

Josh pats Devan's back while nursing his own sorrow. His mind is preoccupied with something other than the sad news. He unsuccessfully tries to reconcile with the preternatural twin occurrences—Rafeena's death on her birthday last year and Wilma's disappearance on her own birthday this year. They both have their twenty-first birthdays on full-moon days. The two tragedies are too eerily similar to be branded as coincidence. They must be planned by the same intelligent mind.

Is his family cursed?

Twenty-one-year-old young women and full-moon nights—Josh repeats the words. A bad combination? Why didn't the tragedy befall the elder sisters Rita and Kareena when they turned twenty-one? His younger sisters Thalli and Curly would be turning twenty-one in just a few years. What would happen to them?

"You are to sleep on the porch like other boys in the family," Thoma says to Jaygust.

The patriarch is mystified by the bizarre nature of the tragedies and figures Jaygust is the culprit.

"It isn't gonna happen," Jaygust says, cut and dry. "Why not?"

"I have been sleeping there. I intend to continue." At the time when Wilma disappeared in 1973, Jaygust turned twenty, practically an adult. It is hard for Thoma to make his son obey him. "Don't you think I am a little boy anymore," Jaygust says.

Kareena and Josh, who have a private conversation about the tragedy, foresee similar fate for the younger sisters. They insist Jaygust move back to the porch. He moves reluctantly.

SIX

FROM RAGS TO RICHES

"This boy is going to live far away from you," the astrologer says immediately after Josh is born.

The astrologer has thick moustache that hangs below the lower lip, masking it. The moustache meshes with the beard, making the combination look like a black beehive.

"How far away?" Ann asks. Like any mother, she doesn't want her children to live far away. She is unsure of the man's watch; how accurate it is. If the time per his watch is wrong, his prediction would be incorrect. The time of the birth has everything to do with the accuracy of the prediction, because the time determines the planetary positions weighing in on the newborn's fate.

"The farthest from you—on the other side of the world," says the man.

"Let me see your watch," Ann is curious.

The astrologer lifts his left arm; he has an expensive Swiss watch.

"See my imported watch? It is very precise," the man declares, putting to rest Ann's hope.

"I'm here at your command, master," Genie announces.

Josh is puzzled. It is the very first time someone calls him *master.* More importantly, he doesn't own Aladdin's lamp, which would invoke Genie. He only has a run-of-the-mill kerosene lamp, a pathetic-looking lamp that has lived long past its lifetime, a run-down lamp beyond its warranty—a disgrace to even Mannuthy's trash pile. It is a lamp far unlike Aladdin's celebrated lamp.

The year is 1975. Josh is at the rental in Mannuthy. He is working on an assignment on the Carnot cycle of Thermodynamics and he intends to burn the midnight oil. When he lights up the lamp, he accidentally rubs on it and the Genie makes his appearance.

"You must be Kerosene Genie, not the legitimate Genie invoked by Aladdin's lamp." Maybe Genie is getting senile in his old age, Josh thinks, making him appear at the beck and call of any lamp.

"Never fear, my friend! I am the genuine Genie—the one and only." "Josh is talking to ghost," Subashini says, broadcasting from her cage in the kitchen.

"Make your wish, master," Genie hurries.

"I want to be out of Mannuthy to study abroad."

Even though Josh had wished to go abroad for higher studies, he realizes for the first time that his wish is ingrained as second nature. His wish came out abrupt and spontaneous.

"Granted," Genie says and disappears in a poof.

The year 1975 marks the twenty-sixth anniversary of his family's arrival at the Mannuthy rental. By now, the eldest three children left home, and his two younger sisters are lost under mysterious circumstances. After he is gone, his parents will be left with the last four of Thoma's love festival with Ann.

The next day, a postman knocks at the door. Josh finds out he is granted fellowship at a Canadian University to pursue graduate program. For Josh, the postman embodies Santa Claus bringing X'mas gift.

Subashini—she of psychic powers—spots the postman coming down the street. She modifies X'mas song and erupts to singing.

> *Here comes postman; here comes postman*
> *With glad news from afar.*
> *His shirt is torn; so are his pants, right down to his shoes.*
> *So is his bag torn at seams with good news, so listen.*

Josh should be happy; Josh should be happy
To hear good news galore.

The postman stashes the letter in the parrot's beak, breaking the song.

The good news spreads across the neighborhood. Josh realizes that going away from Mannuthy is like getting into heaven. India's economic scene is a picture of disaster. The nation fights four wars in a span of twenty- eight years since independence, starting with the Sino-Indian War of 1962, followed by one in 1967. Then there are two wars with Pakistan, one in 1965 and the other in 1971. To many Indians, going abroad is like getting salvation.

He is thrilled at the very thought of traveling to the other side of the globe. It fascinates him to be on the side of the planet where he is awake when India falls asleep and vice versa. He imagines riding above earth on a magic carpet, sailing where feathery clouds silently live, and gliding over continents and oceans into a mysterious land called Canada.

Josh flies from Bangalore to Mumbai with Indian Airlines, and from Mumbai to London with British Airways. From there, Air Canada carries him over the turbulent waters of the Atlantic whose restless waves beat against coastal Canada in their picture-perfect magnificence and heart- warming magnanimity.

This is the very first time he'd flown, let alone taken such an adventurous flight to the farthest point on earth from Mannuthy. Canada is as different from tiny Kerala as could be, a nation as big as a continent, spreading all the way from the eastern Atlantic provinces to the majestic British Columbia on its western Pacific coast; a land defined by the United States to the south and the Arctic Ocean to the north; a land of snowfalls, multiple lakes, vast prairies, and the imposing Pacific Northwest, rightly called a land of supernatural beauty. The profound silence of the unending snow-covered expanse of Canada sharply contrasts with the tiny tropical Kerala.

His feelings upon flying to Canada are like those of his sister Kareena when she traveled to take up a job away from Kerala. She felt relieved that she was escaping to the possibilities that lay outside Mannuthy. He feels that he is in her shoes, except he flies, and she rode in a train. They are, however, in the same boat, being blessed to be let out into the world of possibilities outside their tiny village. He celebrates his freedom just as Kareena did and just as the spirit Ariel did when Prospero released him from the tree he was bound to in Shakespeare's play *The Tempest*.

> *Where the bee sucks, there suck I.*
> *In a cowslip's bell I lie;*
> *There I couch when owls do cry.*
> *On the bat's back I do fly*
> *After summer merrily.*
> *Merrily, merrily shall I live now*
> *Under the blossom that hangs on the bough.*[3]

The genie appears when Josh lands in Canada. "Anything you wish, master?"

"Two things: Success and Happiness."

"Granted," Genie says. "I'm pleased to grant you a third thing: Courage; you'll need it to face a culture shock."

"*Cock-a-doodle-doo!*" chicken crows at the top of his voice back in Kerala.

The renowned Chicken Little from folklore leapfrogs into Mannuthy from another space and time. He shows up at Thoma's rental a few months after Josh left. While merrily feasting on the worms, he remembers that he is not there to have an eating spree and hurries to the task at hand, the one he came for.

"The sky is falling, the sky is falling!" he clucks and clucks, and resumes the worm breakfast.

Thoma, Ann, and their children file out of the rental and gather around the strange rooster. Ann looks at the sky with worried face.

"Get inside the home, everyone," Ann says, hurrying back inside. "Shield your backs from the falling sky!"

With total disregard for the warning issued by Ann, the children spread out to meet and greet the falling sky. Thoma gazes at the sky and then at the rooster. Thoughts of making a curry out of the bird pass through his mind.

Then it happens. The sky starts falling! Chicken Little is pleased that its prediction is materialized. A land of eleven acres falls from the sky. It has a house on it big enough to hold Thoma's family. The vertically falling phenomenon changes its course midway and moves horizontally, landing in Amballore, located fifty miles from Mannuthy.

As detailed by Chicken Little, the property is a gift to the family from Josh in Canada. His graduate fellowship and teaching salary do the trick.

Income barely supports him, so he tightens the proverbial belt to save enough to send to the family. The exchange rate of the dollar is good enough to accomplish the impossible. The newly gained property triggers the family's freedom march, its victory parade, its liberation.

"Thanks to Josh, your family is now able to leave Mannuthy for Amballore," Chicken Little says.

It was all in the stars.

Ann dreamily loses herself to the thought that getting a home is too good to be true; it is a long-cherished dream built over a ladder of time. It beats the wildest expectations everyone dreamed up, and it becomes an astonishing reality at last. To say this is a welcome change from Mannuthy life would be the gross understatement of the century.

Thoma prepares to move out of his island of Elba—his rental home in Mannuthy—to a place where freedom exists: Amballore, his Paris. They are going back to where their ancestry is rooted. Amballore is where Thoma lost paradise twenty-eight years ago. He realizes he is getting a second lease on life. That is what he desperately needed and what Ann had urged God to grant in her daily prayers. At last, they get a place to rest in peace at the end of the day.

They are leaving the very next day on their legendary exodus to Amballore. Thoma loads the household belongings into two bullock carts. The family then eats supper—the last supper in Mannuthy.

It is a full-moon night.

"Thoma, what is that howling sound?" Ann asks at midnight.

Thoma shoots back to the sitting posture on the bed and listens. It is a series of long wails or howls made by dogs and/or wolves. The children wake up.

"Where is Jaygust?" Noman asks, holding up the lit kerosene lamp. The spot where Jaygust slept is empty. They search the entire house, especially the attic. No leads there. They step outside to the yard and guided by the moonlight proceed to the outhouse but can't spot him there. Thoma decides to check out the well in the front yard, but no luck. Kumaran and Bhavany wake up and join the search party.

With lit kerosene lamps held up high, the family walk toward where the howling appears to originate. Thoma instructed all to get armed just in case. They carry butcher knives and sickles from Ann's kitchen. The search leads them to the Mannuthy Municipal Bridge running over Mannuthy River. And then they see the source of the howling: standing on the bridge, gazing at the full moon, and howling wildly, are two wolves.

"They aren't wolves! They are Chettiar and Jaygust," Curly says.

They cautiously walk to the spot, Thoma in the lead. They edge closer, clutching their butcher knives, and take positions on the steps leading to the bridge, ready to run if attacked. Standing close to the howling pair, they identify them: Jaygust and Chettiar! They are frantically howling like two mad dogs.

"Jaygust, come home with us! The man with you is our enemy. He will hurt you," Ann cautions.

Everyone steals good look at the duo. They are covered with body hair all over, including their necks! Their teeth protrude and they have long nails. They look exactly like wolves, except each has two legs instead of four.

The new arrival interrupts the pair's howling ritual, and they are displeased. They jump on the intruders like two dogs. The family runs down the steps to the riverbank. The full moon shines brightly and shows the way.

They look back to see Thoma brandishing a butcher knife at Chettiar.

The wolf Chettiar is much stronger than the human Chettiar and he easily disarms a much stronger Thoma, lifts him, throws him onto the ground, bites him, and scratches him all over the body.

Jaygust is going after the family, chasing them over the riverbank. "Jaygust, it is us, your family. Don't hurt us," Ann and children say while running to get away from wolf Jaygust.

He halts as if he recognizes the voices. He peers at Ann and the rest.

His eyes shift from one face to another in a faint recognition. Then the blank look returns.

"He is in a zombie state," Curly says. "Did Chettiar drug him?" Thalli asks.

A large cloud eclipses the moon, dipping the area in darkness. Jaygust looks puzzled by the disappearance of the moon and stops howling. Standing transfixed on the ground, he is locked in a stare at the absent moon.

This gives the sprinting family time to catch some breath and think of some fresh strategy. They turn around and run in the opposite direction toward the bridge to cross over to the opposite riverbank. While Jaygust stands staring, they run past him. They reach the spot where Chettiar continues to bite Thoma who is now barely managing to fend him off. They run past them, and climb up the stairs to the bridge, run across it, and climb down the stairs, reaching the opposite bank.

In the meantime, the cloud passes, and the moon reappears bright and shiny. Jaygust howls with added vigor at finding the bright object in the sky he lost and regained. He loses interest in chasing the family.

Chettiar abandons Thoma and goes after Ann and the children. When he approaches them, they turn around and swing their knives at him. Chettiar attacks the first in the line, Thalli. He disarms her and carries underneath the bridge, running easily along the sand-filled bank. He disappears under the bridge.

The family sees Thoma rising from where he was felled by Chettiar. His body is covered in sand. They recover their presence of mind by seeing the patriarch back in action, though on the opposite bank.

"Mom, let us go to the bridge; I hear Thalli screaming," Curly says.

Fearing the worst—that Chettiar probably killed Thalli—they run back to the bridge.

"Thoma, come to the bridge," Ann shouts from across the river while running. "Thalli's in danger."

They reach the bridge. Thoma joins them. What they see under the bridge is something they would never forget as long as they live.

Sitting under the bridge is Thalli. She is naked. She sits in a full lotus meditation pose. Her eight arms are spread above her head with their palms facing up, like a giant inverted spider with its legs facing upward. One of the arms holds Chettiar's head, and another holds a bloody sickle, like goddess Bhadrakali did after butchering Asura, the demigod. The blood-submerged and headless body of Chettiar lies nearby naked, with his clothes strewn aside. Thalli sits with her spoil in one of her eight arms, her eyes closed as if in transcendental meditation and breathing deeply.

"Thalli, my darling! What happened to you, sweetheart?" Ann laments when she sees the horror show. Thalli continues to sit frozen without responding. Ann's worry is intensified. She shakes Thalli repeatedly until she is out of her trance.

She opens her eyes and looks at Chettiar's headless body. "You raped my mother once. You now know what it means to rape her daughter," Thalli says to the headless landlord.

Thalli's sari was on the ground. It was wrinkled and torn—the aftermath of the struggle with Chettiar. Ann picks it up, dusts off the sand, and wraps it around her daughter's naked body. The mother is reminded of Thalli as a newborn baby nestled by her side, adorning eight arms, one of which holding Chettiar's head.

Thoma tries to throw Chettiar's head and body in the river to get rid of evidence, but Thalli insists on keeping the head. He must settle for just the body, leaving the head to his daughter. He ties the body to a heavy rock and tosses it into the river.

When the family emerge from under the bridge, they see Jaygust walking toward them. He has stopped howling. They walk toward him and meet him halfway. They are delighted to see he is back to his normal self. The body hair has disappeared. He doesn't have the blank look anymore. He recognizes them all.

"Why are we all here?" he asks.

The family walks back to their home in a surreal midnight parade of eight-armed woman holding Chettiar's head in one arm and bloodied sickle in another, under the watch of a sky full of stars. The full moon shows the way. They have jubilant smiles because they get to spend their last night in Mannuthy rental without the landlord.

Thoma decides that the final resting place for Chettiar's head is the attic he annexed years ago. He hangs the head from the attic ceiling.

"Hang in peace!" Thoma says to the butchered head after thinking against saying *Rest in peace.* *"Now you can watch your rental to your heart's content."*

He exits the attic under a watchful one-eyed Chettiar, closes its door, and climbs down the stairs. He locks the attic door for the last time with a spare lock he has. He takes out the key and tosses it into the water well in the front yard.

The family is up with the lark the next morning. Thoma drives the leading cart. Subashini's cage is hung in front of him. Family chickens and ducks sit in neat cages at the back.

Jaygust drives the second cart. His younger siblings, Thalli, Noman, and Curly sit with him in the rows behind.

Just before taking off, Kumaran, Bhavany, and their two daughters come out to say a final goodbye. They are wearing nightgowns—morning has yet to break.

Bhavany's eyes are teary; she embraces each and every one. "It's about time you meet with good fortune; you deserve it," Bhavany says in choking voice.

"God finally listened to my prayers," Ann says.

"Come back for free haircuts." Kumaran extends standing invitation even though he knows they wouldn't need any free service in the future. "Here, have these," he hands over two bottles of toddy to Thoma. "Come back and visit us."

Thoma pulls into the country road. He is very aware that there is someone in the attic staring down at them with one eye, unable to say goodbye or to come down to give a landlord-to-tenant handshake. "See you in hell," Thoma mutters after turning around and staring at the landlord's final resting place.

"I hope police won't come after us," Ann says. She and the rest must trust they are safe until they are not, until they hear a midnight knock at their new home in Amballore by a uniformed poilceman.

When the twin carts hit the main road after traversing the unpaved country roads, the family knows that a curtain has been drawn behind them, a curtain that closes the final chapter of Mannuthy life. Another chapter opens in front of them, heralding a new life in their Promised Land, Amballore. God finally has taken pity on them by offering a piece of land they could call theirs, and through that piece of land, a long-overdue peace. They need that rare piece of happiness. Ann had been praying for it, but it played hide-and-seek, eluding her, and making occasional cameo appearances. She had been reciting the prayer of Cardinal John Newman when darkness continued to envelop them unfailingly.

> *May he support us all the day long*
> *Till the shades lengthen and the evening comes*
> *And the busy world is hushed, and the fever of life is over And our work is done.*
> *Then in his mercy may he give us a safe lodging. And a holy rest and peace at the last.*[4]

Toma and Ann know that fever of life is not over yet, and their work isn't completed. However, God has granted them peace. He finally picked up the phone when they called him. Through Josh, God has liberated the family from the cauldron of despair. They are at long last, given a safe abode where they can enjoy rest and peace, just as Ann had wholeheartedly hoped and fervently prayed.

It is twenty-eight years ago, in 1947 when India gained her independence from the British Raj, that Thoma was expelled from his ancestral home. He remembers he was a young thirty-seven-year-old man at the time. Now he is making a comeback as a sixty-five-year-old man. "Why do we have meaningless lives?" Thoma asks as if to no one in particular.

"Well, Thoma, my friend, I thought you would never ask," Subashini says. "You might think your life is meaningless—"

"I don't have to think; I know so," Thoma says.

"Life's pains push you to think so, but for you and for those who love you, your life is meaningful," Ann says.

"Life is ultimately meaningless," Tim, Rita's husband, says. He has joined the family in their legendary exodus to Amballore. The English professor quotes from Shakespeare.

Life's but a walking shadow, a poor player,
That struts and frets his hour upon the stage,
And then is heard no more. It is a tale
Told by an idiot, full of sound and fury,
Signifying nothing.[12]

"Life is not meaningless; you add meaning to it and keep on adding till the very last day you are alive," Ann says.

"I disagree," Tim says. "Life's theme is cynical, tragic, and silly." He quotes from Shakespeare again:

As flies to wanton boys are we to th' gods,
They kill us for their sport.[14]

"Let me give you a few lines penned by yours truly on life." Subashini clears her throat, and sings:

Life is a scarecrow in the paddy field
Waiting for you and me to pass by
To scare the daylight out of us
And to laugh out loud when we run screamin'
To our tombs—no better than when we were born.
It is a tale told by clown at blazing bonfire
In the chilling cold of Old Man Winter
About Death Man, who carries us
To the doomed valley of Death.

"Hey, those are my lines, not yours," Tim protests. The parrot doesn't believe in copyrights.

"What we do in a lifetime is so insignificant that only a handful know we even existed when we die," Thoma says.

"In the grand scheme of things, life does not lose meaning because only a few know about us," Rita says.

"Thomas Gray doesn't agree with you, dear," Tim says to Rita and quotes from his "Elegy Written in a Country Churchyard.":

Full many a gem of purest ray serene,
The dark unfathom'd caves of ocean bear:
Full many a flow'r is born to blush unseen,
And waste its sweetness on the desert air.[8]

"Hard to believe that beauty goes wasted because there is no one to enjoy it," Ann says.

"Exactly my thought, mother," Rita says. "Beauty has two elements: objective and subjective. Outside observer homes in on the objective element whereas the owner handles the subjective element. I disagree that an outside observer is the sole judge to assess beauty. The owner has an equal right to do it, if not more."

Thoma's cart belongs to the elder generation and Jaygust's cart houses the younger generation.

The elder siblings believe there is a redeeming quality to the battles their father fought to set things right after he wrecked his children's lives by walking out of the ancestral home years ago, throwing them to the street.

The younger ones form their own family subgroup known as Gang of Four. They don't respect their parents because they don't inspire them. They are critical of the steps Thoma took to bring them up. They believe that their lives are far from a fairy tale, because Thoma was a bystander when they nearly died in the process of living. They are witnesses to life's curveballs their father should have confronted boldly and won over, but instead failed. They believe that their father's retreat was not a tactful one, but cowardly, shameful, and humiliating. He is unlike Julius Caesar who embodies the idea of "He came, he saw, and he conquered." Thoma, on the contrary, owns the idea of "He came, he saw, and he returned." Their father ran away from life's challenges, throwing to winds the inspiration he could have instilled in them.

"My challenges have been many, arrayed in an unending row, impossible to tackle," Thoma protests. "I was dealt an unlucky deck of cards."

Subashini cleans her bright yellow and blue feathers. She munches on the cashew nuts that Kareena brought on her trip to Kerala.

"Your suffering is your own redemption, Father," Kareena says.

Even though he was a thoughtless, heartless, and uncaring person in his younger days, Thoma earns sympathy from his elder children because they believe his punishment was disproportionate to his shortfalls.

"God knows I did my best," Thoma says.

"Glad to hear you acknowledge God, Thoma," Ann is delighted to hear God's name from Thoma.

"Atonement arrived as a late guest in your life, Father," Tim comments. "Better late than never."

Thoma steered the cart carefully, holding the bullock's reins expertly. "We are beggars in the streets of life, and it's because of our parents,"

Thalli says in the second cart. She wears gray sari and a brass ring hanging from her lower lip. There is a reddish yellow bindi adorning her dark forehead. She smokes beedi and puffs out the smoke rings toward the bullocks.

Thalli's resentment-filled statement is literal and symbolic—literal because they were virtually beggars and symbolic because life treated them like beggars, like discards. They were not born with silver spoons in their mouths.

"We are born with wooden spoons in our mouths," Jaygust says while spitting on the bullocks. Those spoons have holes in them, he reminds his siblings—holes that drained out a decent life, retaining rough patches.

"Our father pushed us to poverty," Jaygust continues after sharing a smoke from Thalli's beedi. "He often beat the pulp out of me, and I will remember it always; he is a savage."

"Amen," says Noman, the religious man. He is seated at the back of the cart, slurping on an over-ripe mango. He wears a brown mundu and a mismatching shirt. Thalli and Curly sit directly behind Jaygust. Curly's spread-out hair eclipses Noman's vision of the road ahead. She wears a nylon sari and a matching blouse. Two earrings hang from her ears like two scorned servants.

"To our father and mother, we are like mushrooms," Curly says. "They kept us in the dark and fed us bullshit." The Gang laughs at the joke.

"Praise the Lord," says Noman.

They are determined that their resentment will stay with them even after they move out of the misery-filled rental to the comforts of the Amballore home. Their simmering animosity toward the elder siblings is baffling, as Thoma and Ann think, because the elder ones brought up the younger ones.

The contrast of the elder siblings to Gang of Four reveals the irony of fate, as Ann realizes. There is a role reversal—the elder siblings sacrificed because they had to pick up the tab for the younger ones, and yet they love their parents. The younger ones should acknowledge their father for providing them with compassionate elder siblings, but instead they despise him.

The separation of the elders and the youngster in different carts mirrors their differences in the larger context of life, as Rita and Kareena realize. They belong to two different carts in life: in one, common sense and compassion prevail, in the other, greed takes over. The physical compartmentalization of the traveling family foreshadows what is yet to happen in the future.

The bullock carts crawl along the road at a snail's pace. The sun poked its bright head above the eastern horizon and the road became gradually crowded. Thoma and Jaygust struggle to share the road with faster moving vehicles. With their slow pace, they are estimated to reach Amballore in two days.

At last, the carts reach Amballore.

Amballore citizens give a riotous welcome to Thoma, the prodigal son of Amballore. "Welcome back, Thoma!" they shout.

The new home is located half a mile from Thoma's parental home, where his brother Inasu still lives with his wife Treasa and their children. The property is of trapezoidal shape. A curved secondary road meets the main road at an acute angle and the sprawling yard is bordered by these two roads on its three sides. The fourth border is shared by the graveyard of Amballore Cathedral.

Across from the back fence live Mathettan and Annamma, their close friends from the good old days.

SEVEN

GANG OF FOUR

Jaygust slaps a mosquito sitting serenely on his beard and kills it instantly. He wipes the bloodied hand on Thalli's sari.

"Yuck! Wipe your hand on your crotch," she says, moving away from him.

Gang of Four has deboarded the Kerala Transport bus in Amballore and is walking toward the ancestral home. Noman, the religious crook in the group, rolls a rosary and walks shaking his sagging tummy. Curly sports curly hair braided in pyramidal shape.

Thalli wears a black sari with white ducks embroidered on it in a neat straight line. Her goldsmith husband of the name Cheapsmith employed an expert tailor to make the sari. She wears black lipstick to match her sari.

The Gang is visiting the ancestral home with the explicit purpose of persuading their parents to draft the last will and testament so that the assets would be distributed to just four of them and no one else—a tall order indeed, as they well know.

"Where did you inherit your hair?" Thalli asks Curly. "None in the family has curly hair."

"My beautiful curls are unique to me," Curly says. "No one else has any claim on them."

"I won't call your curls beautiful," Thalli says. "They are more like weed."

"Calm down, girls; no fighting in the street," Noman says. "Praise the Lord."

"Praise your bum, bro!" Curly says. "Why call God all the time? You may as well say 'Praise the Lord' when your wife farts."

"Praise the Lord," Noman says.

The Gang marches over the paved road on a half-a-mile trek, stopping frequently to greet their acquaintances. Thalli's gigantic buttocks gyrate like two sumo wrestlers trapped inside her sari. Little children giggle and make silly bets that the wrestlers would fight their way out of her sari any time.

The year is 1982, the eighth year of Thoma and Ann's stay in Amballore. All the Gang members make good in life—they climb ladders of success and prosperity: university education, employment, and marriage.

Josh paved the way for these, as everyone in Amballore knows. Because the four believe that their good fortunes are what they are entitled to, they are hardly grateful for the good turns in their lives.

"Josh is living in paradise," Jaygust tells the Gang. "He should give us more."

"It's Jaygust who turns his younger siblings against Josh," Thoma says to Ann.

"What does he gain by that?" Ann asks.

"It is his own misinformation campaign," Thoma says. "By ignoring Josh's role in bringing them up, he hopes to mobilize them against him and the elder siblings. Why? Because they are thankless. Also consider it as a sign of revolt by the young and the stupid. Jaygust has made himself the self-appointed leader of Gang of Four, polluting his siblings' minds and putting words into their mouths."

"If his siblings had guts, they would have charted their own course," Ann says. "Blame lies on them too."

"But for Chicken Little, we'll be rotting in Mannuthy," Jaygust says to the Gang while continuing to walk.

"If the sky didn't fall, we would have died in Mannuthy from poverty and desperation," Thalli says.

"All of us saw the sky falling, bringing us property and a house.

Didn't we?" Jaygust seeks assurance from the rest. "Sure, we did," they say.

"Josh claims that he bought the property! Ha-Ha-Ha," Jaygust snorts wildly, sending spittle and snot all around, drowning his sisters' saris.

"Praise the Lord," Noman says.

"Josh deserves gratitude for your upbringing," Ann tells them repeatedly.

"Not him; it is Chicken Little that deserves gratitude," Jaygust corrects her.

"What do you have against Josh and your elder siblings? They gave you a life, for crying out loud."

"That's what they are supposed to do. You and dad should have done it in the first place." Jaygust is quick to blame his parents.

When the Gang reaches home, Thoma is seated in chair, smoking cigarette, and sipping Darjeeling tea. The chair is stationed in the wraparound porch, with Subashini in her cage hanging above.

"Here comes the eight-armed woman with her Gang," Subashini chirps.

"Write the will as I say," Jaygust says to Thoma as soon as they arrive. "Make us four the sole beneficiaries."

"It isn't gonna happen. Keep dreaming."

"Read my lips, old moron! You're gonna hand over everything to us." "What makes you four the sole beneficiaries?"

"Because that's how it is, because we say so."

"If there is one who should be the sole beneficiary, it is Josh.

Don't you forget the property belongs to him." "Amen," Subashini says.

Kuriyan Plamoottil Law Office is by the side of Lovers Lane in Amballore. It is located not far from Amballore High Court. The popular "Judas Toddy Club" is just a toddy-spit away.

It is an unremarkable morning. A bleak gray sky looks on as if displeased with its role of covering the earth.

A big billboard with "Plamoottil Law Offices" written in yellow is stationed outside the building. Statues of two elephants hold it balanced in mid-air with their prominent trunks. Pigeon poop cover many letters. The passersby can make out "moo Law Off" of "Plamoottil Law Offices."

The non-descript building's backyard adjoins a wilderness notorious for its wild animals, a danger to the public. Office is dimly lit, and the passing motorists can hardly make it out day or night.

Twenty-four-year-old Usha is the firm's paralegal for the last two years. She occupies the front office on the ground floor. She greets visitors and sets up appointments. She is beautiful, smart, and intelligent, as anybody can tell who spends a few minutes with her. Kuriyan, the lawyer, is happy he hired her. As a forty-four-year-old man, he finds it hard to keep his dealings with her strictly professional.

"Remember, you are old enough to be her father; no hanky-panky with that girl, you hear?" his wife said upon Usha's hiring.

"Yes, Your Ugliness," Kuriyan said.

It is eight in the morning. Usha arrives after beating the heavy traffic along Lover's Lane. She fine-tunes her makeup using a small mirror she keeps handy. Today's special is darkish-brown lipstick and a matching blackish-brown sari. It is while rubbing her lips together to spread the lipstick that Kuriyan walks in. She is caught with a kissing pose.

"Don't kiss me with brownish-black lipstick; my wife is allergic to it," Kuriyan says.

"Ha-ha. Tell a better joke next time," she laughs artificially. "Your wife is allergic to anything I do."

"Don't let her catch you saying that" Kuriyan warns and heads back to his office with files that Usha prepared previous day.

A man walks into Usha's office. "My name is Jaygust," the bearded man says. He takes out a comb from his shirt pocket and combs his hair, moustache, and beard. He then dishes out a mirror from his pocket and stares at it for a long time, admiring his looks. His bare fingers pluck two of his nose hairs. He doesn't look at Usha the whole time.

"Did you finish admiring your ugly face?" Usha asks.

"I am here to see the lawyer," Jaygust says, still staring at the mirror and ignoring her.

"You need an appointment."

"I have no appointment," Jaygust says. "Instead, I have disappointment; I am disappointed at your law office."

"You must be a nut to say so," Usha says.

"Your lawyer drafted an illegal will per request from my father, Thoma," Jaygust explains. "I want to talk to him." He proceeds to Kuriyan's interior office.

"Sir, you can't walk in without appointment."

Kuriyan hears Usha. He cranes his neck out through an open window and sees a short man heading toward his office. Usha is in hot pursuit with a sari held in her hand. "What does she plan with the sari?," he wonders.

Usha spreads the sari by holding its ends in her arms and hurls it in front of her like a fisherman would cast a net to catch fish. Her aim is right on. She traps Jaygust in her sari and holds him in a stranglehold made of sari loops she makes with lightning speed around his neck, like a magician would make a rabbit out of a handkerchief.

"Usha, is this how you catch men?" Kuriyan's words are mangled by his uncontrolled laughter. "My wife never had to cast a net to catch me."

"Let go of him," Kuriyan says when he realizes that Usha has no intention to let go of the man.

"Next time, I'll send you to your grave," she says after releasing him. Jaygust catches his breath and walks into Kuriyan's office.

"You can't let my parents draft the will the way it is," Jaygust says. "They have to give the whole property to us, the youngest four in the family."

"Find another lawyer; I represent Thoma," Kuriyan says and leads him outside the building.

The Sunday gathering of Gang of Four is to plan out some things.

Jaygust arrives first. He doesn't stop by the host, Curly, who meets him at the door. He zips past her, straight to the kitchen, and dips into the frying pan, picking up hot sardines with his bare hand.

"Don't eat them. They are still raw," Curly says.

Jaygust stuffs three sardines into his mouth and gorges on them, to the disgust of Curly and Frankie, her husband.

"I prefer uncooked sardines," Jaygust declares.

Curly is dressed in a yellow sari and has a matching yellow bindi on her forehead. Her hair is in unmanageable disarray, crowding her scalp like weeds that grow abundantly in her yard. She has yellow lipstick and has colored her eyelashes in repulsive yellow.

A knock at the door. In comes Thalli.

"Look who is here," Curly announces loudly. "It is the ugliness incarnate."

"You look gross," Thalli says to Curly. "You don't look great either," retorts Curly.

Thalli is dressed in a black sari with little white ducks embroidered on it, her favorite outfit. Her breasts stand out in front of her like two huge bodyguards ready to kill anyone who messes with her.

"Your coconuts are growing out of control," Curly points her fingers at Thalli's breasts.

"They are much better than your puny mangoes." Thalli almost touches Curly's peanut-sized breasts while pointing at them.

"Praise the Lord," says Noman, the false prophet, who walks in. "Which lord are you praising, your brother Jaygust?" Thalli mocks.

Noman follows Jaygust's advice on anything. The sisters believe he worships him.

"Noman regurgitates Jaygust's words," Curly says.

"I must say Noman is just lip-synching; Jaygust is who does the talking," Thalli says.

The girls talk among themselves often to the effect that Jaygust is a ventriloquist and Noman his puppet.

"It is Sunday. If you haven't been to church, at least praise the Lord," Noman says.

"Praise your bum," Thalli says.

Frankie prepared a sumptuous lunch. He wears a checkered yellow brown mundu and a red T-shirt. He sports a long moustache, not because he likes it but because Jaygust ordered it. Frankie asked Curly not to join Gang of Four, and this displeased Jaygust and he in return ordered Frankie not to shave until further instruction from him. This resulted in an enormously long moustache that stretches like a country highway. The moustache droops below his chin, and scares away little boys and girls.

The Gang members meet in a room adjoining the formal dining room.

They sit around an elegant marble table with an ornamental chandelier hanging above. Frankie stands nearby like an obedient butler whom everyone calls Jeeves, including his wife.

"Tell us about your plans," Thalli asks her two brothers.

"We are to break into Kuriyan Plamoottil's Law Office building. His office holds the will," Jaygust says.

"How safe is it?" Curly asks.

"Safe or not, we have to take a chance," Noman says.

"The office is spread over the first floor and the second floor: I had an opportunity to check it out when I visited the other day," Jaygust says.

"Kuriyan's paralegal is a monster; she almost strangled Jaygust," Noman says.

"Let us hope she won't be there during the break-in," Curly says. "She won't be," Jaygust says. "Our operation is at night."

The sisters assign the brothers the break-in task, planning behind the scenes and guiding them.

"Do we know if the upstairs and downstairs offices are interconnected?" Thalli asks.

"They are connected by stairs," Jaygust says. "Downstairs is inaccessible from outside because of a locked gate."

"Our plan is to get to the upstairs using a ladder and jump onto the balcony," Noman says. "From there, downstairs is accessible."

"Then what?"

"Take a photocopy of the will." "Will that be enough?"

"We will learn of the contents, including the will executor appointed by the testator Thoma."

"I see why you need to identify the executor. He is the keeper of the will's original," Curly says.

"Exactly."

"Details like how many copies exist and which institutions keep them are not important, as long as we identify the executor."

"Then what?"

"We will replace the lawyer's copy exactly where we found it and vacate the premises."

"What are the future plans?"

"Alter the contents of the executor's copy to make us four the sole beneficiaries."

"Intriguing plot for a plot of land!" Curly uses rhyming words. "Yup, it is," Jaygust agrees.

"Praise the Lord," Noman says.

Jaygust and Noman get off the auto rickshaw past midnight. After making sure the vehicle sped away, they enter the law-office complex of Kuriyan Plamoottil. The moonlight guides them. The plan of the two brothers is to break into the law office.

"I took a mental picture of the complex when I came here last week," Jaygust says. "I have a pretty good idea of the building layout."

"Give me instructions; I'll follow them." Noman is Jaygust's follower.

Earlier in the day, the two brothers surreptitiously hid a foldable ladder on the premises. They planted it inside a bush in the wilderness right behind the building, out of view of the passing motorists and pedestrians.

"There it is. Just the way we planted," Jaygust spots the ladder. They retrieve it and walk back to the building. Time is the key, Jaygust reminds his bro; they need to complete their stealthy mission the sooner and get out before someone gets suspicious and calls the cop. It helps the brothers that it is the dead of the night, and all of humanity is sound asleep.

Once at the building, they unfold the ladder and lean it against the back wall. Noman stands on the ground to hold it while Jaygust climbs up. So far, so good and all according to the plan, the brothers agree.

"I'm glad we waited for the full-moon night," Jaygust says while climbing up. The light comes in handy to communicate in sign language to avoid being overheard. He reaches the second floor, alights from the ladder onto the balcony that leads to the office window. His plan is to break the window and get in.

"Your turn!" Jaygust signals. "Come up, bro. I'll secure the ladder at the top."

Noman climbs, taking his sweet time and carefully scanning the surroundings to make sure the bright moonlight doesn't give them away.

Noman, however, does not reach the second floor. Someone watching the clandestine operation intervenes. That someone has been watching them from the wilderness. It is a gray wolf, also known as timber wolf.

The animal stealthily approaches the thieves and topples the ladder by jumping up and slamming against it. The ladder loses balance and swings.

Its tip comes down, describing a giant arc, with Noman perched atop. Noman screams as he rapidly plummets to the ground. As soon as the ladder contacts the ground, Noman wiggles out of the ladder and runs. "Run, bro, run," Jaygust directs from the top.

The wolf has a partner in crime. It is its brother. The principal attacker joins hands with the associate wolf and together they chase Noman who is struggling with his pendulous tummy. He begs his tummy to run with him, to help him out, but he is met with insubordination by his body part. It charts its own course of action, bouncing left to right and top to bottom. The insurgency slows down Noman's forward motion.

"Run faster," Jaygust prompts. "You should have exercised to keep in shape." The advice comes belatedly as the brothers now realize.

The wolves catch up with Noman. The attack comes with lightning speed. As soon as they fell Noman, they roll him onto his back, punishing his attempts to stand up by biting him and scratching. They stand on their hind legs, propping their front paws on the fallen man's paunch. Wolf One is stationed on the left side, and Wolf Two on the right. This bilateral vigilance blocks Noman from rolling away to escape.

Without wasting time, they bite through the fat belt that buffer belly muscles. The fallen hero screams in panic and pain.

"Where is the beef, bro?" Wolf One asks the other. "What do ya mean?" Wolf Two asks.

"I'm getting only fat. Where is the meat?"

"Ya just read my mind. I wanna bite into real flesh too." "No lean meat on this fatso."

"Ditto here, dear bro."

"Let's hope our next meal will be real."

With salivating mouths, the four-legged brothers send hungry looks toward the victim's evil brother atop the balcony.

"That meal on the balcony looks like lean meat," Wolf One says between slurps of Noman's semiliquid fat.

Jaygust is frozen in terror. He pees profusely in his mundu while watching the bizarre feeding ritual between two talking wolves. He shouts at the fallen brother to get up and run. Noman continues to lie down, unable to extricate himself from the grips of two clever wolves. He is blood-splattered and semiconscious.

Noman had previous plans to undergo liposuction to drain out belly fat, but he didn't get around doing it. Now, miraculously, two four-legged surgeons perform that procedure in the operating room of the night. A full moon glows like the high-intensity lamp of the operating room and the surgeons are assisted by several nurses in the form of countless stars scattered over the infinite sky in the profound silence of the night.

The wolves howl at the full moon, giving up the fruitless feeding session and go back to the building. "We have the rest of the night to get you," they inform Jaygust.

Being a wolf of sorts himself, Jaygust understands their language and howls back, "If you think you can outfox me, think again. I'm the cleverest fox around."

As the night wears on, the wolf pair and the human wolf continue playing the waiting game. Both teams are sure of their stamina and will-power to outwit the other. Wolves realize that when the morning breaks in the good old east, it would be too late to hang around; they must retreat to the safety of the wilderness. Urgency is of essence.

"Hey, bro, what do ya think?" Wolf One says. "The man atop is a wolf 'cause he is howling at the moon. He looks evil too."

"He is bad like us," says Wolf Two. "No. He is worse," says Wolf One.

For the first time during their midnight mission, the wolf brothers look scared.

The standoff between the wolf brothers and Jaygust prevails for long time. Jaygust is in a vulnerable position, being stranded atop with no rescue in sight. His partner in crime, Noman, has been grounded. The ladder is out of reach, making it impossible to reach the grounds.

But the immediate business is to get the will, and that too, before the night wears off. Soon the town will be waking up, the milk trucks will be in the streets, and boys on bicycles will be delivering *Amballore Times*. He must act alone—his helping hand is probably dead.

He walks around the balcony. The frame of a window is warped. There is a small opening between the window and the wall, giving direct access to the interior. If he can access the hinge through the gap and throw it back with a twig or stick, he is in business. He leans on the balcony and plucks a tree branch and carves out a thick stick. After fiddling around with the hinge for a few minutes, bingo! He throws the hook back and opens the window.

The wolves watch the clandestine operation with a mixture of confusion and fascination. Jaygust gets inside the law office illegally.

"Did we lose our lean meat dinner?" Wolf One asks as Jaygust disappears into the room.

"He is out of our watch, but not out of our reach," says Wolf Two.

Jaygust turns on the interior light, ready to turn it off at the slightest provocation. He strides through the interior keeping an eye out for any unexpected person. If he meets someone, he plans to bail out of the room, scramble down the jackfruit tree, dodge the wolves, sprint like hell to Lovers Lane, and get lost in the grand disarray the highway is notorious for.

He searches the filing cabinet holding files in alphabetical order. The letter T appears. He gets hold of the will and painstakingly goes through the contents, absorbing the details and making notes. He places the file at its location and hops out through the open window.

The wolf brothers are relieved to see him. "When're you coming down?" they ask.

"Keep dreaming," Jaygust says.

He mentally maps out his course of action for escape that involves overcoming several hurdles, planning to cross each bridge when he comes to it. He is not inclined to rescue his brother, which will delay the escape. He has already accomplished the goal of his nocturnal mission and letting Noman bleed to death is something he has no qualms about.

Jaygust gathers valuable information. The will's executor is South Amballore Bank. The will inside the bank vault is the official one that is presented for probate. This is the one that the courts go after if the will is ever contested. If there is disagreement between the official will and Kuriyan's copy, the official will prevails.

Jaygust decides to go after the bank's copy and alter its contents to suit the interests of Gang of Four. But that is a task for another day.

"Then you'll know who is the smartest," he howls to the wolves.

They are keeping vigil on him. He plucks a jackfruit, cut it open with the knife he carried, and starts eating his breakfast while sitting in the crook of the tree. He tosses the jackfruit nuts to the waiting wolves.

By now, faint streaks of sunlight start spreading around.

"I will outmaneuver you both. Watch me," he informs the wolves.

He decides to sit out the waiting game. Some more moments pass, and the sun starts peaking from the edges of horizon. The wolf brothers know they are at the end of the game. They dodge the brightening daylight and quietly retreat to the safety of the wilderness, giving up their plan to eat Jaygust.

"*Adios, amigos* (goodbye, friends)," Jaygust howls to them in Spanish.

Usha reaches the law office at the crack of dawn. She lets in fresh air by opening the windows and doors of the downstairs offices. These consist of Reception, Waiting Room, Kuriyan's office, and Client Consultation Rooms. She walks upstairs to do the same. It has file rooms and large conference rooms to accommodate corporate clients. She walks down the balcony surrounding the upper offices.

She stops dead in her tracks. Looking out into the grounds, she spots something there. In the morning fog, she can't make out what exactly it is.

"Kuriyan, come here," she screams.

Kuriyan hikes up the stairs and comes running. They gaze curiously at the mysterious object.

"It's someone sleeping on the ground," Kuriyan says. "Maybe a homeless man." Usha notices something about the man—a reddish mess around him. "He is bleeding."

When they approach the scene, they see a bleeding man, probably dead. They suspect he is a robbery victim. Upon further examination, they find to their horror that his tummy has been ripped open.

"The stomach is not penetrated," Usha says. "Outside skin and fat deposits are torn open." There are deep scratch marks on his face and body. His clothes are ripped open.

"The bleeding is extensive," Kuriyan says. "Victim of animal attack. Scratch marks are telltale signs."

The lawyer and the paralegal sit around the victim to take closer look.

Usha checks the body for heartbeat and breathing. "He is alive," she declares.

"I recognize this man! I have seen him somewhere," Kuriyan says, staring at Noman's face but still not connecting. "Maybe he is a client who got attacked on our premises."

Usha pulls out the man's wallet and examines the contents. It is filled with rupee notes.

"Animal attack all right," Usha agrees. "Not a robbery victim." Which thief would rip someone's tummy sack, deplete its fat, and leave without taking the wallet?

"The animal must have gorged itself on the man's fat and left without killing him," Usha says.

"A generous animal," Kuriyan notes. He is not sure if a wild animal, most probably a gray wolf, an inhabitant of the wilderness behind his law office, would do such a thing. They usually kill the victim and then devour it. Wolves do not like moving parts attached to the body they were devouring; they expect the victim's total submission.

"I wonder if the animal dragged the victim to our premises or he happened to be here when attacked?" Usha asks while examining the wallet and pulling out ID. The lawyer examines the photo and the name and hits the roof. The man has the same last name as Thoma, who recently drafted his will in his office.

"He has resemblance to Thoma; maybe his son?" Kuriyan wonders. "No wonder I thought I saw him somewhere."

"What a strange name to have. *Noman*. Not a man?" Usha bursts into laughter despite the grave circumstances.

It doesn't take too long for them to put things together. They are aware that the younger siblings protested the will. Noman's presence at the law office under suspicious circumstances can't be accidental.

"Was he trying to tamper with the will?" Usha asks.

"Probably," Kuriyan says. "But then he comes under animal attack in the process."

"Serves him right," Usha says.

"Animal attack fizzles his plan," Kuriyan says. "Either that or he was attacked after the will tampering."

"He doesn't carry the will," Usha says after examining him further. "Usha, check our files to see if Thoma's will is missing," Kuriyan says. "Check to see if there is any sign of trespass into our office."

They then did a Good Samaritan's job of calling the ambulance. The ambulance carries Noman out of the law-office complex to the emergency ward of the Amballore General Hospital.

They find no evidence of forced entry into the building. Jaygust did a good job of covering up any evidence. Thoma's will is intact and unmoved from the file folder. This leads them to believe that the animal attack took place prior to the attempted robbery. The culprit was on his way to their office when the animal inttervened.

Kuriyan presses charges against Noman, claiming he infiltrated the Law Office complex with criminal intent. The charge lands Noman in Amballore Jail immediately after he was released from the hospital.

"Fight your case. The lawyer has only circumstantial evidence against you," Thalli and Curly say to Noman. But he decides not to since it would implicate Jaygust and expose the Gang's wider scheme of infiltrating South Amballore Bank vault to falsify Thoma's will.

Noman becomes a formal jailbird and wears the prison uniform—a striped mundu and red shirt. He sports a beard that grew since he was taken to the jail, since shaving is disallowed there. He sports a thick bandage around his stomach.

Jaygust visits Noman on his last day at the jail. He stays outside the cell at the visitor's spot and Noman stays inside in shackles.

"I am carrying the cross for you," Noman says.

The crooked elder brother smiles with pride. He has executed a perfect crime, leaving no trace of trespass. His spineless brother—that is what Jaygust calls Noman—deserve to be jailed.

"The easiest way to access the vault is if you are a bank employee," Jaygust informs.

"But we are not bank employees," Noman points out the obvious. "How do we get our hands on the will?"

Neither brother has any background in finance or accounting. The only financial background of Jaygust is stealing money Josh sent to the family.

"Maybe we can apply for janitorial jobs," Noman suggests. He adds that janitors can access any nook and cranny of the bank, spy on the workers, and access the code to get into the vault.

"Moreover, I have a background in information systems. This will enable me to unravel the code," Noman says.

Accordingly, the brothers form a fictitious janitorial company called *Brooms for Hire* after Noman is released from the jail. "We will clean for you while you sleep," the ad boasted. They contact South Amballore Bank and offer their services for reduced rate. Both are called for interview.

"How much experience do you have with cleaning?" the bank manager asks. He presides over the interview board, which consist of senior bank officials. He sits at the head of a marble table in the bank's formal conference room. The two brothers sit at the other end. They are nervous.

"I've used brooms to beat my father and mother," Jaygust says.

He has been warned in the confessional stand at the local church never to lie during a job interview. The parish priest insisted on this when Jaygust asked him if he could lie about his background in janitorial services. "They have ways of finding out the truth if you lie," the priest warned him.

Noman looks embarrassed by his brother's reply, but to his and the interview board's surprise, the manager bursts into laughter upon hearing what he thought was a joke from Jaygust.

"I like your sense of humor," the manager tells Jaygust amid the surprised looks all around him.

Brooms for Hire is hired to meet the cleaning needs of South Amballore Bank. It doesn't take long for the evil brothers to find the code to the vault and access the will. Jaygust replaces it with the one he'd prepared. Per verbal agreement with other members of Gang of Four, he was entrusted to distribute the property equally among the four of them and was expected to draft the will accordingly.

Did he do that? Did he comply with the common agreement? Why did he not share the contents of the falsified will with the rest? Did he pull off some treacherous act by which he was immensely benefited?

The bank lays off *Brooms for Hire* few months after the company was hired. It comes to the bank's attention that Jaygust has been beating his mother and father with brooms meant to clean the bank building. This is in direct violation of the cleaning contract.

It was a no-brainer that the company was fired—not that the brothers cared to keep the job. They had accomplished their goal.

EIGHT

DEATH MAN COMES KNOCKING

Thoma collects a deck of cards, which was gathering dust. Once upon a time, he made a living by making Subashini pick the cards to predict people's fates. The cards were put away when Subashini started making erratic predictions.

"Predict when I'm going to die," he says to the parrot, spreading the deck.

Subashini drops the peanut she is munching and picks a card. The card predicts the imminent death of Thoma.

"You are giving wrong prediction as before," Thoma protests. He is, however, worried.

Subashini's prophecy confirms a certain palm reader's foreknowledge about Thoma. He met the palm reader at the famous Trichur Round. "You don't have much of a future," the palmist said to Thoma, pointing to the disappearing lifeline on his right palm. Thoma refused to pay the palmist in protest. Ever since the prediction, he stopped seeing traveling palmists who come by his home.

Adding to this alarming situation is the instance of an inexplicable photograph taken during the wedding of his youngest daughter, Curly. The bride and the groom, Curly and Frankie, are seated on a pedestal on the wedding stage. Thoma and Ann stand by their sides. The studio photographer clicks the scene.

The photo is of high quality. However, there is something odd about the picture: instead of the expected four people, there are five, including a ghost standing behind Thoma. The ghost appears to hold Thoma by his shoulders, as if to protect him from an impending disaster. Thoma's gaze is focused on a distance and is riveted by a bizarre scene—a raging inferno of hell.

"The ghost is your guardian angel," Ann tells Thoma when she opens the envelope the postman delivers and sees the photo.

"Thoma is to go to hell; that is why he looks terrified," Annamma, the neighbor, says.

"No," says Ann. "He is assigned the Hell by mistake; his guardian angel is restraining him."

People who attended the wedding remember that Thoma was smiling when the picture was taken. In the photograph, though, Thoma is nothing like how he was when snapped. There is not a trace of a smile, just terror.

"Maybe the negative was improperly developed," Thoma remembers Curly saying.

"Maybe a spilled curry gave rise to the artifact," Noman suggested.

The lens quality becomes a suspect. However, the photo studio confirms the lens is impeccable.

"Maybe the chemicals used are faulty," Ann said.

"The answer is negative, ma'am," The studio said. "Our chemicals are without blemish."

No other picture taken during the wedding has this sort of anomaly.

No other person photographed on the happy occasion had an altered appearance in the photo. No one else had a ghost protectively holding him or her.

This incident added credibility to the widespread speculation that there is an impending tragedy in Thoma's life.

The picture starts changing as the days go by, adding to the alarm it already caused. Different scenes start popping up. It is as if the changing pictures narrate a story through its evolving content.

An additional entity appears one day in front of him: a devil with two prominent horns on its head and a long-curled tail. The new arrival looks menacing. Thoma is caught between the ghost behind him and the devil pulling him to the hellfire. The devil points his index finger, which has a long nail, toward a fiery path to the hellfire. A signboard appears at the end of the path. It says, "To Thoma's eternal damnation."

The ghost's hold on Thoma weakens as time progresses. The devil wins the tug-of-war with the ghost. One day, the devil carries away Thoma and his guardian angel, the ghost, disappears.

Then it happens. The picture starts making sounds. The sound effect starts with frightening laughter. The laughter becomes more alarming, getting louder as the days go by. It changes into a hum of garbled sounds. Spoken words emerge. There is a one-way conversation between the devil and Thoma.

"Come to the eternal hellfire, Thoma; we'll keep you warm for eternity," the devil says.

The talking photograph becomes a full-fledged movie. In the movie, the devil shows Thoma how the inhabitants of hell are suffering. Then there appears a chilling scene where Thoma is engulfed in hellfire. He screams.

While this drama is going on, the other side of the photograph shows that Ann is also destined to end her days on earth. It shows that an angel escorts her to heaven. On the day when hellfire consumes Thoma, Ann is shown being inducted into the halls of heaven.

Then the movie stops. It becomes a still photo of raging fire. There is no one in the photo, just the fire.

On the last day of the hell-bound transformation, the photograph starts walking. It raids the bedroom where Thoma and Ann sleep.

"Wake up, Thoma. You've slept enough," it says.

"It's not morning yet," Thoma tells Ann, wiping sleep from his eyes and gazing at the alarm clock. It wasn't Ann who was talking; she is lying snoring by his side.

"Hey, look at me!" Thoma hears someone say.

He turns on the light and sees a fiery photograph trekking across his bedroom and heading toward him.

"Your days are numbered. Ha-Ha-Ha!" the photo says.

Then it burns out and perishes, spewing black smoke and ash.

As Thoma ages over the years, job seekers line up to be recruited to move in with him. Mr. Arthritis is in the front of the line, followed by Mr. Diabetes, Mr. High Blood Pressure, and Mr. Parkinson's Disease. Toward the back of the interview line stands Mr. Stroke followed by Mr. Heart Attack. The last candidate is Mr. Lung Cancer, who keeps on smoking and coughing intermittently.

"Stop smoking," Parkinson's Disease, shaking with tremors, shouts. "Stop shaking," Lung Cancer retorts.

All candidates break into laughter.

"My joints can't stand the pain," Arthritis says.

"I'll do anything to have a transplant," Heart Attack says, clutching at his heart.

"How sweet you are, sugar man," Blood Pressure compliments Diabetes.

"Thank you, Your Highness Pressure," Diabetes says, sending another round of laughter.

Soon, a fight breaks out between Stroke and Lung Cancer.

"I can paralyze you instantly," Stroke boasts, pushing back at Lung Cancer.

"Don't you forget that I am the most sinister of us all," Lung Cancer claims, sending his smoke rings at Mr. Stroke.

"Easy, folks! No fighting," Thoma shouts at the warring men. "I'll kick you out if you fight, then you're on your own, out in the street for good."

Thoma hires all the applicants. They move in with him, crowding his body like guests of a cheap motel.

Arthritis constrains Thoma's movements. He becomes a diabetic.

Heart problems run in the family. He is struck with a stroke that paralyzes part of his body. He develops a hunchback. He can hardly walk.

He uses a cane to get around. He walks regularly around the neighborhood to get the old blood flow going and to get badly needed exercise. He becomes wheelchair bound. Josh sends him a state-of-the-art motorized wheelchair from Canada. It is a heavy-duty robotic wheelchair that can be mobilized, restrained, and steered with analog and digital controls that sit at his fingertips. It has four robust tires and can pick up speed of twenty-five miles per hour.

Ann is still healthy enough to manage the housework by herself. Their lifelong friend and most precious child Subashini is still with them. They needed no other bliss in their retirement, Thoma assures Ann.

It was just the other day when a ghost flirted with her. What happened is almost laughable, she was quite sure. She was leaning over the red brick wall which bordered the cemetery, watching the dying embers of a funeral pyre when out from the ashes came a ghost with devilish laughter. She was about to turn back and head out to her kitchen when he called out to her.

"Ann darlin' don't go away."

"Don't call me darling; that is for my husband to say," she protested.

"When you get to know me, you'll change your mind," the ghost said, licking his mud-smeared lips and baring its moth-eaten gum and spit- smeared hanging teeth. "Be forewarned of *Death Man* who'll pay you a visit soon."

"Who is he?" Ghost got her attention.

"He is coming to take you to Heaven," he said, scratching his left arm pit with ugly looking fingers. When she hurried back home, he cried out in a shrieking voice, "He will take your darling husband to Hell."

Ann talked to Annamma, her confidant and neighbor, about the troubling encounter. "I am seventy years old. Who in his right mind wants to flirt with me?"

Annamma considered the question seriously for half a minute and passed her verdict.

"Only a ghost would." The two septuagenarians burst into laughter.

A powerful wind blows from the neighboring graveyard and whooshes past the trees outside her kitchen and topples plantain trees. The windowpanes tremble in the windstorm. The slanting rays of the afternoon sun percolate into the house.

Ann licks the clay pots clean to savor the remaining bits of curry. It is her time-honored ritual to give the pots a tongue cleaning prior to water immersion, which rechristens them for the next meal.

At that moment, a demonic laughter rings out from the graveyard. It is an unnatural sound — a howl and a laughter admixed, a blood-curdling growl, an infernal shrieking, a belching loud like monsoon thunder; in short, a cacophony of damned sounds hailing from the center of hell. Its viciousness paralyzes her with terror. She drops the clay pots, breaking them into many tiny pieces.

"Thoma, are you OK?" she cries out, thinking Thoma was howling. He has been turning insane as advanced age nonchalantly marches through him. Is dementia preying on him, creeping on him like a sneaky snake? Once a paragon of good health, stamina and great looks, her husband is now anything but.

She runs toward Thoma, stepping over the broken pots. What she sees puts to rest her worry: Thoma is dozing peacefully on the porch in the outdoor hallway, his feet stretched and resting on a bamboo chair. Above him in the hanging cage sits Subashini, their beloved parrot.

"Thoma is sleeping," the parrot announces.

Ann takes hold of the hand fan and drives away a mosquito that settle on Thoma's forehead.

If the graveyard ghost is right about their imminent deaths, she is left with only few days with him, and this saddens her. She has known him for half a century. It was a giant leap of faith for her to tie a marriage knot with him, an unknown man who came to her life in an arranged marriage setup. However, she trusted that her marriage was made in heaven just like the priest who officiated their wedding said in Amballore Cathedral years ago. And yet it wasn't an easy marriage. Far from it. But she is convinced that he made amends for the failures he orchestrated. Even though he crashed the plane and all but orphaned his family, even though he unfailingly failed to be a husband and father, even though he provided no shade in the sun and no umbrella in the rain to his family, he tried to be a man of principle. He failed to hold on to them at times because God singled him out to send a truckload of problems his way and consequently his motivations were derailed, and courage depleted. He could not carry on wearing the armor of principles when realities confronted him with their cold-blooded stares.

"A lot of women would have run away from hm," Annamma said to her.

"My love for him is unbreakable," Ann said. "Our love is toughened by hardships and sacrifices."

She learned no to pass judgment on her husband's character flaws and mood swings. She erected a formidable edifice at the border of faith and reason and stayed firmly grounded on faith never crossing over to reason; if she did, she would long have given up on him. Despite numerous setbacks in the form of challenges and pitfalls in their married life, she cultivated reinforced conviction that their alliance is predestined.

Not that there were not moments when she tended to agree with Annamma, a saintly woman like Mother Teresa, who would raise her impassioned arguments against Thoma for a reason. But she knew in her heart of hearts that her heart belonged to Thoma, come what may. The challenges and hardships were sent their way to test their endurance and make them stronger like blazing fire cleaned gemstones making them shinier. They endured challenges in the raging waves of life, coming out victorious and their bond fortified by the test of time. At long last, in the evening of their lives, she is at peace with him.

A ghost stands at the graveyard gate, staring at Thoma and Ann. He is holding a soccer ball.

"This is for you," he kicks the ball. It vaults over the fence, bounces off the ground, and rolls toward where the Thoma is stationed. The ghost is gone.

"Remember me?" the ball asks Thoma. It has a thundering voice which belies its small size. Thoma and Ann look at each other and then at the incredible talking ball.

"I am your friend," it says, standing steady. It appears to stare at Thoma who is numb with uncertainty, his silver-streaked hair reflecting the afternoon Amballore sun, making him look like an old saint with silver halo. He kicks a chair toward the soccer ball, sending it flying.

"Ha, you missed!" the ball mocks, moving away from the flying chair. "Don't forget, you are no more a young man with clear aim."

The ball undergoes a transformation. It starts manifesting eyes, nose, mouth, and everything that makes up a human face. In few minutes, it becomes a full-fledged human head with a grin. It rolls toward the hedge at the entrance to the outdoor hallway.

It manifests a small body underneath the head, and it rises swiftly. In no time, the whole body and four limbs are in full view, and they define a tall creature with menacing look.

He steps over the hedge and comes close. Then they recognize him. It is good ol' *Monsoon Man* who used to invite himself to Thoma's Mannuthy rental during monsoon seasons.

"The devil has come back," Subashini announces.

"Don't sit there staring at me," he says to Thoma. "Talk to me, my friend!"

"You aren't welcome here," Ann says. "Go away!" "Go away," Subashini repeats.

"As if I needed a welcome!" the creature says, grabbing the fallen bamboo chair and taking a seat across from Thoma. He wears shoes made of snakeskin. He is clad in a black-and-white robe—black on the left and white on the right. He has yellow eyes. Even though he gazes at Thoma he isn't making eye contact, his piercing stare blazing straight through him and resting on the plantain tree behind Thoma.

"Get out of here!" Thoma screams.

Ann grabs the cross hanging on the wall and flashes it in front of the intruder, hoping to drive him away. He pulls Ann by hair, snatches the cross, and tosses it.

"Your end is near," he says to them. "I'm here to take you to your ends."

He then tosses a card to the couple. Ann picks it up. She reads her obituary on it. It startles her to realize that she is going to die on that very same day.

Thoma examines the card after putting on his glasses. He flips the card and reads the other side. His obituary is written in bold letters. The funeral details are inscribed on it. Written on it is the date he would die—that same day! It is August 3 of 1988, the peak of harvest season and couple of weeks ahead of Onam festival.

Death Man, having sown seeds of terror in the old couple, heads toward the lone coconut palm by the side of the outhouse. He continues to grow taller by the minute. His black-and-white robe stretches behind him like a bride's gown would span a long line of pews on her way to the altar. The moment he reaches the palm, he stations himself there. He is now as tall as the tree.

His robe elongates as he becomes taller, keeping pace with him. He looks like a gigantic scarecrow. The crows take off in a panic, their frantic wingbeats speaking volumes on the terror he instills.

The news spreads around Amballore that an apparition has appeared in Thoma's yard and is stationed there to fetch them to their afterlife. Curious crowd arrives and they watch in awe Death Man growing taller.

"It sure isn't a ghost, not a devil, nor is it a spirit," one man says. "Call it Black-and-White Movie," says the other, looking at its black-and-white robe.

The good neighbors Mathettan and Annamma pay a visit. Annamma plans to drive the spirit out using a rosary that the archbishop of Amballore Cathedral had blessed. Ann is happy to see her good friend and confidant.

"Is he the Antichrist?" Ann asks Annamma.

"It won't surprise me," Annamma says. "Look at the world we live in. It is so sinful that the Antichrist's arrival is imminent. The end of the world is here!"

The two women approach Death Man, kneel in front of him with their arms stretched. "Begone, devil! Leave us alone." These women are famous in town as saints, and their prayers are expected to have results.

With the crowd kneeling and praying, Thoma's home turns into a shrine.

There is a rush. The crowd makes room for the vicar of the church. The spectators realize the situation has reached a pivotal point, serious enough to bring a priest into their midst. The godly man sprinkles holy water on the creature. Death Man growls in protest.

The night is fast approaching. People lit candles and the yard glows like a miniature Milky Way.

They say their final goodbye to the couple. "Make room for us when you reach heaven," they say, hugging Ann.

Ann knows these are the final embraces and they signal the inevitable death soon to come. Thoma releases Subashini from the cage. "Good-bye, my friend. My best friend," Thoma says.

"I'll meet you in my next life. So long!" Subashini says and flies out to the top of a plantain tree and then disappears from the scene.

Thoma feels pain in his heart when Subashini leaves.

He feels more anguish at the thought of losing Ann forever. During rare moments of introspection in the past, Thoma has felt that Ann is a saintly woman naïve enough to put her faith in the goodness of human nature.

Therefore, she trusted him and chose him as her husband. He doesn't deserve her. She is embodiment of human kindness, emblem of infinite fortitude, and token of unassuming humility. Some part of him knew that Ann is simple enough to put unshakable faith in the wreck of a man called himself, despite him landing her devastation and destitution ever since she cast her lot with him. However crudely he might have treated her, he could not have carried his cross without her. She has been his cheer leader all along. There are moments when he agreed with his heart when it told him that he loves Ann, unbelievable though it sounds to the rest of the world. He doesn't believe in heaven; but he believes that his marriage to Ann is made in heaven. He and she, opposites to one another, have been pitched in a bondage and this is the stuff unusual stories are made of.

The worry that he is going to lose his soulmate for good distorts his face with agony.

"It is time to go," Death Man announces in a hoarse voice. He produces two sacks: a white sack from his right pocket and a black one from his left.

"I am making two deliveries today. I will carry Ann to heaven in the white sack." He waves the white sack.

"The second delivery is Thoma, and I will carry him to Underworld in the black sack." He waves the black sack.

The crowd gathers around Ann, forming a thick layer of humanity blocking Ann's capture. Another crowd gathers around Thoma.

Thoma stands up from his wheelchair and waves away the encircling crowd, clearing a path. He moves forward with his walking stick, calm and steady. When he reaches Ann, he stops, drops the cane, and embraces her. His eyes are wet.

"Thoma, we will never meet again. We are going to two different places. I am sad," Ann sobs. "But you'll always live in my heart."

"You'll live in mine too," Thoma says. "No one can take you from me."

The palm tree nearby bends a little closer to listen to their conversation. "Why do we have sad lives, Thoma? Why does life end up in tears?"

"Life starts with birth which triggers happiness," Thoma dips into Greek mythology. "But it's a misleading prelude to the ultimate tragic end when Charon ferries the soul across Hades."

"Maybe we can come back as spring flowers in the next life," Ann says. "Or as stars in the sky. They're happy always."

"I don't mind leaving this meaningless life," Thoma says. "When you're gone, I'll miss the meaning you gave to me."

"This is the hardest thing I will ever do: leaving you," Ann says with tears trickling down her cheeks. "Will anyone remember us after we're gone, Thoma?"

Thoma says to Ann that even if no one remembered them after they are gone, the centerpiece of their existence consisting of love, faith, and failed pursuits of happiness will survive as a testament to the meaning they gave to their lives.

"Sure," Ann says, "It is sufficient to build a lasting memorial in our own hearts. We won't need anyone remembering us."

Death Man pulls Ann from Thoma's embrace, lifts her up, and drops her in the white sack and deposits the sack in his right pocket.

He does the same with Thoma, depositing him in the left pocket. "Good-bye, Thoma and Ann," the crowd weep.

Death Man becomes very asymmetric by now. His waist is some hundred feet up, but upward from the waist he is disproportionately tall. His head reaches the invisible milestone way up in the sky. His upper body encompasses the solar system. His face becomes invisible.

He walks toward the graveyard, sneezing periodically and breathing like a thousand beasts roaring at the same time. The earth rumbles when he moves and trembles when he sneezes. It moves out of its orbit with every step he takes. He crosses over to the graveyard.

He lifts his right arm, grabs sun from the evening sky and brings it to earth. The evening turns bright like noon. Many Amballoreans die in the scorching heat, and some turn blind. He swings his gigantic arm and throws the sun, sending it to where Pluto orbits. The town freezes in the instant winter that ensues.

Ann looks down from Death Man's right pocket. She sees an ocean of lit candlesticks held by the crowd like the light assembly of Diwali, the Festival of Lights.

Death Man, now with his face near the planet Neptune, heads toward the graveyard entrance. His robe becomes heavy as if made of lead. The crowd makes room for him. Some gets trapped under his feet. He tramples on tombstones, his robe sweeping them up like a sprawling broom into a heap. Corpses come out screaming from underneath the tombstones.

When he reaches the entrance, he takes off skyward like a rocket carrying a satellite. The trio is propelled outward to the outer fringes of solar system and then far beyond. They mesh into the deep void of infinity.

Amballoreans look up into the night sky until Thoma and Ann disappear.

"Thoma is seated in the wheelchair at his home, just like when he was alive," Varkey informs his drinking buddies of Judas Toddy Club. "The chair is stationed on the wraparound porch. Remember the spot where he used to sit when alive?"

"Of course, we do," they say.

"Does he stare at a distance like he used to do?" Markey, Varkey's wife, asks.

"He does. His gaze is focused on the tombstones in the nearby graveyard. He is drinking his favorite drink, toddy," Varkey says.

"I think he wants to guard his home," Patro says. "Why else would he come back?"

"How about coming back to drink toddy?" someone answers.

Laughter makes rounds.

"The only thing different now is the parrot's cage. It is no longer there." Varkey said.

The patrons at the neighboring table pull their table and join the group.

"Don't you folks know that Thoma was here just the other day?" Yohan from the new group asks.

This fresh news causes gasps of surprise. Many jaws drop. "What was he doing here?"

"Same as what we all do, drinking toddy." A chuckle goes around.

"Just like when he was alive, he wheeled himself into the club," Barbas says. "Earlier, he was unable to get to the second floor. But not anymore, thanks to some gadget the chair is retrofitted with."

A murmur goes around on the need for an elevator for wheelchair access.

Barbas continues. "The new wheelchair defies gravity; it floats and lands at the head of the stairs. He wheeled himself to us. This gave me a start and I dropped my bottle."

"Tell us what happened next," Varkey prompts.

Barbas refuses to be hurried. He sips toddy in slow motion and munches fried sardines with green pepper pickle, taking his own time. After downing the mouthwatering dish, he continues. "Thoma joins us as if it is normal for a dead man to visit a toddy club. While we look at him in stunned surprise, not sure if we can talk to him or even get a reply from him, he places his order.

"'Judas,' he calls out. The club owner doesn't hear him. 'Judas,' he bellows out for a second time. Judas looks at Thoma and is overwhelmed by horror at seeing a dead man and drops expensive Johnnie Walker bottle.

"'The usual.' Thoma places his order and joins us at our table. "Judas immediately fetches his *usual*: fried prawns, boiled tapioca, and toddy. Thoma takes a long draught of toddy as if he hadn't touched the stuff while away and now is making up for the lost time. He eats the fried prawns and tapioca with relish, as if he had been on starvation diet. He doesn't utter a single word, as if we didn't exist. We sit around him in astonishment, too unsettled by seeing a ghost drinking toddy.

"I summon the last grain of courage I have and say, 'Thoma, talk to us.' But the man doesn't budge, too absorbed in drinking.

"Judas comes around and refills Thoma's plate. He takes out a fresh bottle from his tray and offers it to Thoma with his arm stretched out, but he is such a nervous wreck at serving a ghost that he trips on himself and bumps Thoma's body.

"You won't believe what happened next—Judas's arm goes straight through Thoma's abdomen and penetrates his back, the arm still holding the bottle. 'Serve the toddy in front of me, not behind,' Thoma shouts, making us roar with laughter.

"After the drink, he wheels himself to the stairs. We follow him. The wheelchair rises by itself and moves forward, gliding over the stair steps.

"We climb down in pace with him."

Barbas takes a sip and continues. "At the stair landing, the chair turns around and continues to descend. When it reaches the ground floor, it floats over the floor and heads to the exit. The exit door opens automatically even though it isn't an automatic door. Once out of the building, the chair touches down and stays there for a moment.

"All of a sudden, it takes off. It soars high like a kite. The moon is shining, and we can see the wheelchair flying in the tranquil night sky against the backdrop of countless stars. It ascends the soft clouds and disappears."

NINE

SÉANCE

"The coffin dodger finally croaked," Jaygust announces.
Gang of Four receives the news with cheers. They are meeting at Curly's home.

Coffin dodger is Gang's nickname for Thoma, coined for his unpardonable crime of being alive and keeping at it. They would rather he quit doing it.

At last, their wish comes to fruition.

The ringleader of the Gang, Jaygust, arrives unshaved. He has a walking stick replacing his lost left foot; sometimes he uses crutches. He lost his left foot when Thoma shook him off coconut palm into the shit pile of the outhouse. Thoma's memorable words to him at the time he dipped in the brown stuff has kept ringing in his ear ever: "*I always knew you are full of shit.*"

"At last, the wrinkle face can officially rot," Thalli chimes in. "Praise the Lord," Noman says.

Thalli shed a gallon of crocodile tears when she heard the news, covering her face with a pink handkerchief on the pretext of wiping off the tears, but underneath the towel she smiled sumptuously and snickered satisfactorily.

"Jesus listened to my prayers," Noman says. The religious man goes to church daily and prays for the destruction of his enemies, which include his elder siblings and parents. He habitually holds the Holy Bible against his heart while reciting enemy-destruction chants.

Curly says nothing, but there are no tears in her deep dark-brown eyes. There is no trace of sadness on her pale-brown face.

Noman has recovered from the wolf attack six years ago. The fat deposit depleted by the attacking wolves has been replenished by a new supply. His midriff is once again buffered by semifluid fat that is bubbly like a girlfriend he has a hard time getting rid of. It moves around him like a rooster making a mating dance around a hen.

As usual, they meet in the large downstairs conference hall. Curly's colonial mansion is in the outskirts of Amballore. She and Frankie purchased the nineteenth-century mansion just after they got married. The mansion has the pleasing British architectural style modified to include elements of Dravidian architecture, which include sandstone and granite. The house has a vaulted roof and wide doors, which gives it an open-air feeling matching the tropical Kerala climate.

The news of Thoma and Ann's disappearance has a palpable presence in the room—not a mournful presence as would naturally be expected among deceased parents' children but a celebratory one. The reactions from Thoma's family are mixed. The elder siblings are saddened at the sorrowful news and feel guilty they were absent when Death Man made off with Thoma and Ann. Gang of Four, on the other hand, partied overnight by visiting Judas Toddy Club and getting drunk head over heels.

They are aware that the realization of their dream of getting the property title is at hand at long last. They look forward to the splitting of the loot among just the four of them—*loot* and *spoils* are the terms they use to refer to the property. The curtain drop they wished to happen just happened: Thoma and Ann are gone. They believe that the property had fallen in their laps when Chicken Little cock-a-doodle-dooed outside their Mannuthy rental. Now is the time to lay their hands on the property.

Jaygust already contacted Kuriyan Plamoottil, the lawyer entrusted with the will, and delivered the news of death. "The old man and Ann have finally croaked," he said. "It's time for the property distribution."

"The process will get rolling once I get the official death certificates," Kuriyan said.

Amballore Times refused to print the obituaries of the elderly couple because their dead bodies could not be located. There was no documentary proof of their death, no signed and validated death certificates from any doctor, medical examiner, or coroner. The Birth and Death Registry in Amballore declined to issue death certificates in the absence of proof of death.

"A huge crowd of Amballoreans were present when Death Man eloped with the grave dodgers, and that is proof enough they died," Noman says.

"I think Josh staged the whole show," Thalli says. "Death Man is someone he sent from Canada to snatch Thoma and Ann, I am pretty sure."

"Why would he do such a thing?" Curly asks.

"Josh's scheme is to send a huge Canadian man he cleverly disguised as Death Man," says Thalli. "He engineered the plot to make Thoma and Ann disappear without death certificates, depriving us of our inheritance." "I knew all along that Josh is a big schemer," Jaygust says.

"And a crook too," Thalli adds.

"Have no fear, folks!" Noman says. "There is a way to prove Thoma died."

Everyone's eyes turn to Noman. "Tell us," they scream all at once.

"I propose we hold a prayer meeting where I will invoke the spirits of the dead," Noman says. "If Thoma makes appearance, it is proof he is dead. If he doesn't come to the séance, it means Josh is hiding him in Canada."

"The Amballore Police is at fault for not arresting Death Man, an intruder from Canada," Jaygust says.

Frankie comes around carrying a tray with tea and *idlis*. They call him Curly's husband because no one felt like wasting a name on him. However, as time rolled on, he was called Frankie. He still sports a long beard and moustache, having been forbidden to shave by an order issued by Jaygust.

The beard reached his belly button, and the moustache grew long like the unending beach along the Arabian Sea. Curly hates to see the hair outgrowth and requested Jaygust to lift the shaving embargo, but the ringleader sticks to his rule as if it is a *fatwa*.

Frankie does not join Gang of Four to plot stealing of Thoma's Last Will and Testament to alter its contents. Nor does he lay blame on Josh and Thoma for family problems, a fact-challenged accusation the Gang proposed and nurtured. That is reason enough for Jaygust to outcast Frankie and impose shaving embargo on him.

"I much prefer toddy," Jaygust says when Frankie offers him tea. He tosses it toward the window, smashing the window glass. Frankie brings the alcohol as demanded. He cleans up the spilled tea.

Thalli orders toddy and drinks it with relish, making big slurping noises. She eats idlis voraciously as if it is the first time she dips into those delicacies. She belches loudly, making Curly close her nose in disgust.

"If that son of a bitch Josh planted a Canadian imposter on us, I will strangle him," Jaygust says, farting ferociously.

"Ew! Go easy on the beans, bro," Curly says, and turns her face away from him.

"Frankie, get me toddy." Curly places the order.

"Yes, ma'am," Frankie says. That is how he addresses his wife—*ma'am*.

Curly knows she is lucky to get him as her husband. He is an expert chef and worked at a local restaurant prior to becoming a nurse. He cooks the meals for Curly and their two little girls. He is the last child in his family consisting of fifteen boys. His father made a fortune collecting dowries for his fourteen boys. When Frankie's turn came, Curly refused to give dowry. "If you demand dowry, you can kiss our marriage off," Curly said. "Yes, ma'am," Frankie agreed. Curly has a sneaking suspicion that tables could have been turned to make him pay dowry to her, but she didn't push her luck too far.

"If Josh's agent kidnapped Father and Mother and left them in Canada, we can get them back," Curly says. "They don't have Canadian visas. Josh will be in legal trouble for kidnapping and giving asylum to two Indians."

"Praise the Lord," Noman says.

The Gang decides to reconvene to perform the séance.

When they assemble at night in the majestic meeting room, the lights are turned off and candles lit. The statue of Mahatma Gandhi stands at the corner watching the ceremony. Noman, the religious swindler, leads the séance.

"Praise the Lord! Let destruction visit upon Josh," Noman says the preliminary prayer.

Everybody repeats. Jaygust and Thalli skip the "Praise the Lord" part and jump right into "Let destruction visit upon Josh."

Noman had instructed them to keep off alcohol and come to the gathering with a clean mind. Jaygust and Thalli stole toddy from Frankie's fridge and sneaked it to the séance.

"My dear brother and sisters," Noman addresses the fellow crooks with sober voice. "We are gathered today to talk to our beloved father."

Jaygust and Thalli laughed aloud at the qualifier *beloved*.

"He has either died or been kidnapped by Josh. Let us hold hands and invoke his spirit."

Jaygust holds Thalli's hand. She holds Noman's hand, and he holds Curly's. Curly holds Jaygust's hand to complete the circle. They sit around the marble table and pray in silence, with a glowing candlestick atop the table. Its flames flicker in the eerie silence. Frankie lingers in the pitch-darkness of the surroundings, ready to serve food and drinks.

Noman looks toward heaven and rolls his eyes, so much so that only the whites are visible. He starts talking in gibberish. Between the long streams of rubbish from his fat mouth, he adds brief proper phrases, such as "damnation to Josh" and "massacre of elder siblings." Jaygust is delighted to hear these heart-warmers. Thalli and Curly chuckle and pray.

"Shut up, you motherfucker."

The booming voice erupted from inside the house and gives everyone a start. The marble table rises in the air and lands with a heavy thud. The supplicants holding hands scramble. Noman wets his pants. He stops praying per the command from the invisible whomever. All of them gaze toward Frankie, wherefrom the thundering voice originated.

"It is not me, sir," Frankie says to Jaygust, who looks at him accusingly.

Frankie's German shepherd barks ferociously at him, an unusual thing for the loyal dog to do. Something is wrong.

"Listen, you all," the voice continues. "you bastard," (Addressed to Jaygust, who is biological son of Chettiar, not of Thoma), "you eight-armed bitch" (To Thalli), "you fat-belly," (To Noman), and "you weed-hair." (To Curly). "You can shove the property ownership dreams up your asses for all I care. I refuse to die."

Thalli turns on the light. There is no doubt now—Frankie is talking to them. He talks in a thundering voice, unlike in his usual soft voice. They figure someone is speaking through him, using him as a medium. The stream of expletives from his mouth is a testament to Thoma's identity. Frankie never curses because he knows Curly would kill him if he does so.

Jaygust breaks the stunned silence. "If you aren't dead, you won't appear at our séance."

"I'm the living dead," Frankie says. "I'll keep on living to deny you ungrateful weasels your inheritance."

"You shot yourself in the foot, old fart," Thalli says, looking at Frankie. "All we need is your appearance at our gathering. We tricked you to do just that. Now we know you are as dead as a plank of wood."

"Praise the Lord," Noman says.

The Gang talk among themselves in whispers. They agree that perhaps Thoma took the initiative to disappear and die away from Amballore, leaving no evidence of death, to deny them their inheritance. The man staged his own death. "The old man had an arranged death, just like he had an arranged marriage," Jaygust jokes, but nobody laughs.

Curly has difficulty talking to Frankie as if he is Thoma and not her husband. But talk she must, she knows.

"Did Death Man carry you away from earth?" Curly asks. "Ask your mother's ass," Frankie answers.

Under normal circumstances, Frankie would not dare speak to his wife rudely, but the poor man is under siege. They needed no more evidence to prove that Thoma is present at the séance. (Who else would say *your mother's ass*?)

"May I serve you more toddy?" Frankie asks the Gang. He is back to his normal self. He looks confused and tired, as if energy is drained from him.

Thoma's powerful yet invisible appearance rudely interrupts the Gang's meeting, but now they are back to normal. But not for long.

Thalli started swirling. She spins three times and stops. Then she speaks —in a masculine voice, a very thunderous masculine voice. "You bastard!" she addresses Jaygust. "I'll make sure you get no property."

She then shoots up in the air as if from a springboard, vaulting herself with her body held horizontally. She is like an agile teenage gymnast. Thalli aged thirty-three—she of five feet and 250 pounds—moves with incredible speed. Feet first, she kicks Jaygust in his midriff so powerfully that he flies from where he is sitting, collapses against the wall with chair in between, slides down, and is grounded. She follows her prey like a tigress, and with supernatural strength, lifts him off the floor and bites him around his neck. She then rattles him, gripping him by her powerful jaws like a fox would hold a chicken. After a few waggles, she spits him out toward the chandelier. His head smashes against the chrome finishing of the ornamental lamp. He collapses on the marble table.

Noman, who invoked the spirit, sprints in panic.

Thalli goes after Noman, catches up with him, trips him, and places him on his back. She jumps up and down, up and down, on his gigantic tummy like on a trampoline. She lifts him up with just one hand. "You are greedy like your bastard brother; you don't deserve my property." She then carries him back to the meeting room and flings him toward Mahatma Gandhi's statue, breaking it into pieces.

By now, her energy is depleted; she looks exhausted. She sits at the marble table with right elbow resting on it and holding up her head. Thoma has left her.

Suddenly, Curly howls. She wobbles.

"You bitch! You're no better than your crooked brothers," Curly says to Thalli.

She pulls on Thalli's hair, drags her off the chair, lifts her with singular strength, climbs on the table, and ties her to the ceiling fan by hair. Thalli hangs like a three-dimensional scarecrow cartoon drawn by a mischievous artist. Curly turns on the fan at full speed. Thalli goes round and round as the fan revolves.

As Thalli circles round and round, Curly sings nursery rhyme in a masculine voice:

> *The wheels on the bus go round and round*
> *round and round,*

round and round,
The wheels on the bus go round and round
over the city streets…

Thalli's skirt spreads wide and wide as she goes round and round, exposing her fat thighs and unshaven legs.

Curly is exhausted. She rests at the table.

Frankie gets back into action. He starts barking very loudly, scaring the bejesus out of Curly, who has recovered by now. The German shepherd barks with its master, giving Frankie moral support. Frankie crawls on the floor on all fours like his dog and snarls and barks ferociously. His head turns in all directions like an owl. He jumps, lands, jumps, and lands. He then moves toward his wife with lightning speed, springs forward, bite her weed hair, and pulls it off her head.

Curly sits at the table and weeps in shame when her husband or rather Thoma exposes her baldness in public. Only Frankie was privy to the secret that she camouflages her bald head with weed-like hair. Her bald head shines in the chandelier light with sweat overflowing and dripping onto the marble table. Her wig has been caught in Frankie's mouth.

One week passes since Thoma and Ann disappeared from the face of the earth.

Ravanan, the probate lawyer of South Amballore Bank, sits at the mahogany desk in his large office located along Lovers Lane. He is a thirty- eight-year-old bachelor and has been with the bank for a few years. He has important visitors that day—Thoma and Ann's children are expected.

The bank is the testators'—the elderly couple's—designated trustee institution and is entrusted with publicizing their will when they decease. It falls on his shoulders to read out the will's contents when the children arrive. A sealed envelope containing the official will rests by his side. It has been retrieved from the bank vault just a few moments ago. The children will at last know what Thoma and Ann planned with their estate.

Gang of Four already knows of the will contents. Or do they?

He looks forward to meeting the children, but more importantly, he is excited about seeing his heartthrob, the thirty-year-old Usha, the paralegal of Kuriyan Plamoottil Law Offices. She is expected to arrive in the company of Kuriyan, the testator probate lawyer representing Thoma and Ann. The trustee bank has invited him to be present when the will is read.

Ravanan tidies the heavy-set whiskers on his face with a comb. He massages his moustache upward with his bare fingers and makes sure his headful of hair is combed upward, the way Usha likes. He is named after Ravanan, the ten-headed demon king of Lanka in Indian mythology. Usha calls him *demon*. She does not want to worship Ravanan, the demon god, but she loves the lawyer Ravanan.

Kuriyan and Usha arrive. The lawyer comes with his copy of the will, which he carries in a sealed envelope. The lawyers are required to check that their respective wills are identical.

"Where are your nine other heads?" Usha asks Ravanan, referring to the legendary demon king.

"Oh, them? I sent them in search of you," Ravanan says.

She wears a purple sari with ten-headed Ravanan embroidered on it.

She wears thick brown lipstick and has matching nail polish. She has shoulder-length hair. Ravanan isn't sure who/which is more beautiful, she or her sparkling diamond nose ring.

Her effervescent personality is what attracted him to her more than her arresting beauty. What intrigues him is her smile—an opulent, full-throttled, open-hearted, and lavish smile which makes him worship her in his heart's atrium. When beautiful women smile at him or laugh, it is as if he is getting invited to their bedrooms. But Usha is different, her smile puts to rest the cares of life and offers an alternate universe of tranquility. Her smile is more than the facial tissue redistribution it causes. An unknown language is needed to describe it.

Kuriyan knows his paralegal likes Ravanan, and they are romantically involved. As for him, his wife has forbidden him from fooling around with his beautiful paralegal, threatening him with increased rib bones in case he dares to do so. He stays put, only passing occasional comments on her makeup and hairstyle.

"Yours is an intriguing romance—Usha's one head against Ravanan's ten heads. Ten for one," Kuriyan says.

"It takes Ravanan's ten heads to match my one head," Usha says, pointing to her head and shaking it provocatively. Her neatly arranged hair sways tantalizingly, so thinks Ravanan.

"On the other hand, you need to reincarnate ten times to match my brain," Ravanan boasts.

"It's just demon talk, darling," Usha says to Ravanan.

One by one, Thoma's children start dropping in. Rita and Tim arrive first.

"Our condolences to you two on your loss," Kuriyan says. Ravanan and Usha convey their sorrows. Rita's tears drop. She is in mourning phase. She wears a black sari to commemorate the dead. A black bindi adorns her forehead.

"My father and mother are irreplaceable," Rita sobs. She uses a black handkerchief to wipe off the tears and to blow her nose.

"My in-laws are very ordinary people but extraordinary in some ways," Tim says.

"Between them, they contributed 150 years to this world. That alone is an accomplishment," Kuriyan observes. Thoma was seventy-eight, and Ann seventy-two.

The rest of the children arrive. Jaygust arrives first, followed by Thalli, Noman, and Curly. George and Kareena arrive. Josh is in Canada and can't make it. As for the other two children, Rafeena is deceased, and Wilma disappeared long ago.

Several chairs are placed around the desk. Everyone takes a seat.

Jaygust sits alone and away from the rest. He picks his nose and plucks nose hairs with bare fingers, spraying them on the elegant mahogany desk. He smiles broadly, with his upper lip moving leftward and the lower lip rightward, creating a comical face. No one knows if he does this deliberately or if there is an anatomical anomaly that creates the nauseating asymmetry. He is delighted to see the familiar-looking envelope that sits by Ravanan's side. He also recognizes the envelope that Kuriyan holds in his hand, which, as he knows, contains the text different from

Ravanan's official copy. The disagreement doesn't matter though. The will of the trustee (South Amballore Bank) is the official one and what matters, and that is the one that lies by Ravanan's side. He could hardly wait for the fireworks to begin.

It is the trailing phase of the monsoon season and there is rain beating against the windows. The morning sun peeks from among the gathered clouds like a child playing peekaboo. The slanting rays illuminates the office. Long-leafed fans hang from the ceiling, making whirring sounds.

Fluorescent lamps shine overhead. A swarm of little flies frantically move around the lamps, terrified by the fan-driven bursts of air.

Tim, Rita, George, and Kareena huddle together. They sit away from the younger ones. It is clear the two groups move in different circles; the elders keep to themselves. For them, the tragic demise of the elderly couple is too much to bear. Rita said to Tim that the dynasty is winding down, giving room to a new generation. "Life is nothing, but a series of concatenated plays enacted by generations after generations," Rita remembers Tim telling her. She is often the privileged recipient to the wise quotations from Tim, the English professor.

Thalli, Noman, and Curly sit together in their own group. Thalli has dense formation of dirt under her nail, but she hides it cleverly with thick black nail polish. She is dressed in a colorful nylon sari with numerous multicolored flowers printed on it, resembling the flamboyant painting of the Grateful Dead, the famous American rock band. She wears a single yellow trumpet flower on her sumptuous black hair. She is hardly dressed for the occasion; her gala outfit, suitable for a carnival, stands in sharp contrast to Rita's mourning outfit, a simple black sari.

"Jaygust deserves thanks for executing our plan," Noman whispers, referring to Jaygust's feat at will alteration.

The Gang members remember the plot they masterminded and successfully executed six years ago in 1982. Noman and Jaygust created a fraudulent cleaning company and planted themselves in South Amballore Bank to access and falsify the will. At the mission's end, Jaygust told them that he included just the four of them as the beneficiaries of the altered will. The trio love their leader, Jaygust, even though they know he is a duplicitous crook.

"Come sit with us, bro, don't be a stranger," Noman invites Jaygust. "I'm OK here." Jaygust prefers sitting near the lawyers to get a closer look at the forged envelope, his handiwork. His speech is slurred because of a premature stroke due to heavy drinking. When he said *I'm OK here,* the assembled people heard *I'm with a whore.* Usha's high-pitched laughter rings out.

The trio of Thalli, Noman, and Curly expect the will to allocate the whole inheritance to just the three of them and Jaygust. That is what Jaygust told them as how he forged the will, and that is what they believe. They expect to hear, "We bequeath our plot of land and house to our youngest four children. With love, from Thoma and Ann." They remember the words by heart. Why not? Were they not reciting it in their minds for the last six years? The signatures of Thoma and Ann will attest to the authenticity of the will, but only they know that the forged signatures are inserted by Jaygust.

How delightful it is to see the elder siblings are excluded from the will; the Gang gloated. They waited to see the letdown that would soon discolor the faces of George, Rita, and Kareena.

Jaygust salivates at the happy contents to become public soon of a short will made up of two sentences: "We bequeath our plot of land and house to our beloved son, Jaygust. With love, from Thoma and Ann." That is how he drafted it, but he knows that other Gang members, his sidekicks (as he calls them), think it is different. Let them think so, he doesn't care. He waited to see the devastating blow to visit upon his partners in crime. His elder siblings, especially that son of a bitch Josh, will be disappointed that they are excluded from the will. Thoma and Ann's voices will speak from the grave to deny all his worthless siblings—even his younger ones—the inheritance they built their dreams on.

"We will know soon," Jaygust loudly declares this double-edged sentence to no one in particular. The lawyers look at each other and then look away. The Gang members laugh happily. Noman's horse-laughter sets in motion his gigantic tummy that moves up and down, shaking the mahogany desk. Curly laughs mildly while massaging her weed wig. She still carries in her heart the humiliation when Thoma exposed her secret during séance, that she was bald and wore a wig.

The door opens. A uniformed court official enters the room, a very serious-looking gentleman. With him is a menacing-looking tall security guard. He is six feet nine inches tall, an unusually tall Malayali, as unusual as a man on Mars. He bends down to clear the arched doorway, and now stands erect after entering the room, dwarfing everyone assembled. He has fierce eyes. His movements appear to be programmed; he walks like a robot with hesitating motion, not continuous like a human being. He bows in front of the gathered crowd, but his spine refuses to bend fully. The official takes a seat at the head of the table, near the lawyers. The robot man, also called Goliath for his extraordinary height, stands behind the lawyers and stares blankly in front of him. Thalli and Curly giggle at seeing this supernatural ape.

Ravanan calls the meeting to order. "I know you are here with sad hearts at the loss of your parents. I formally convey my condolences to each and every one of you."

"The offices of Kuriyan Plamoottil Law practice convey our sincerest condolences upon your tragic loss," Kuriyan says.

Usha nods her pretty head in agreement.

Rita and Kareena sob. Usha comes around and console them, wiping their tears with a soft tissue. The lawyers and the paralegal are not surprised at seeing the younger siblings with stone faces, unconcerned at the loss of their parents.

"Let us start this meeting with a silent prayer for the deceased," Ravanan says.

All stand up and observe one minute of silent prayer. Jaygust and Thalli struggle to contain their insane laughter at the thought of praying for their parents, a laughter that takes root in the pits of their stomachs, ready to burst out "Let them rot in hell. Praise the Lord," Noman prays.

After the prayer, everyone sits down. Ravanan delve right into the task at hand. He opens the envelope. Kuriyan and the court official witness this act. He reads the contents. "We bequeath our plot of land to all our children, to be distributed equally. In addition, we bequeath the family home to Josh. This is in recognition of his selfless love to provide a home to his siblings. God bless him. With love, from Thoma and Ann."

That was it; it was a short will. It was short and sweet, but short and sour to Gang of Four. They sit in stunned silence, dumbfounded. They can't figure out what went wrong. They look at each other in disbelief, and Jaygust stare at the lawyers, astounded. Thalli sits there with her mouth wide open, unable to suppress her surprise.

"Give me it," Thalli suddenly stands up.

She moves fast, reaches the head of the table, and grabs the will. The robot man, Goliath, gets hold of her hair, toppling her yellow trumpet flower, and drags her back to her seat while retrieving the will. He goes back to his post and resumes staring at the thin air.

"Only I deserve to get the property," Jaygust stands up.

The Gang members get confused at his claim to the entire property. "I say the will is rigged," Noman says, concerned at the inclusion of the elder siblings. He struggles to stand up but fails because the desk blocks his tummy. He keeps on sitting.

The lawyers congratulate all the family members. They compare their wills once more and affirm that the contents are matched. The court official concurs. They let the children inspect both the wills.

"We don't want to inspect," Curly says. "We know the will is rigged." "How is the cleaning business, folks?" Ravanan asks Jaygust and Noman.

Most of the audience is lost at this strange question. The brothers look at each other.

"Haven't you heard about the bank's hidden camera?" they ask, breaking into wild laughter and sending knowing looks to the two brothers.

The Gang now know what happened. "They watched us and caught us in our act and kept it a secret, giving us false hope. Let curse visit upon them," Jaygust and Noman would pray next Sunday at the church.

Ravanan takes out an envelope — the falsified will drafted by Jaygust.

The Gang leader doesn't need to open it to know the contents. He already knew. However, the rest of the Gang read its contents. "We bequeath our plot of land and the house to our beloved son Jaygust. With love, from Thoma and Ann."

They can't believe their eyes. "You snake! You traitor!" they shout at Jaygust and storm out of the probate building. Jaygust, their so-called benefactor brother, has stabbed their combined backs. He would have become the sole beneficiary of the will if the bank hadn't installed a hidden camera in the vault. Camera is their friend now, which caught their ringleader red-handed in the act of forging the will.

There is poetic justice to the whole story, as the lawyers note. The Gang tried to backstab their elder siblings by excluding them from the will, and now one in the Gang does the same to the rest.

The court official declares the meeting can't proceed because of insufficient quorum after the three siblings stormed out of the meeting. "The meeting will resume on another occasion," the serious looking court official orders.

TEN

SOMNAMBULISTS

"Even though you are the beneficiaries of the will, we have a problem," Ravanan informs Thoma's children the next day when they resume the interrupted meeting.

"Now what?" Gang members call out all at once. They bit the bullet just yesterday when they realized the property had to be shared among eight of the siblings, not just four of them. The new development adds insult to injury.

The Gang made up after the previous day's feud. Thieves always stick together, through thick and thin.

"We have no proof that Thoma and Ann died," Kuriyan says. Usha is seated near him and takes down the notes diligently.

"Since there is no proof of the testators' death, the will cannot be executed." Kuriyan delivers the bad news. Loud gasps and angry shouting from the Gang members fill the room.

"All the citizens in Amballore know Death Man kidnapped them and took them to outer space," Jaygust says, standing up.

"I totally agree with my brother," Noman says, sitting down, trapped by his belly blocked by the table.

Usha roars with laughter at the mention of *Death Man*—it is the first time she hears of such a man. Goliath laughs with a booming sound—it took some time for him to catch on. When the serious-looking court official sends a sharp look at the guard, he applies a sudden break to the laughter and this results in snorting sound.

"Describe to us *Death Man*," Ravanan asks.

"He was so tall that his head reached the planet Neptune," Thalli says.

This statement triggers laughter from all the assembled men and women, including the sober-looking court official.

"Is it Bugs Bunny who greeted the head when it reached Neptune?" Ravanan asks. "Or is it, Santa Claus? It could even be Mickey Mouse, you know." The robot man's baritone laughter and Usha's high-pitched laughter sail across the law office.

But the Gang members do not laugh. Instead, they look at each other in confusion. "It was all in the news; check *Amballore Times*," Thalli says.

Gang of Four had bought the newspaper carrying the news of the elderly couple's disappearance. Curly phones Frankie to bring her copy.

"I am breaking the session until newspaper arrives," says the court official. He phones the offices of *Amballore Times* and orders the back-dated copy. The clerk from the newspaper delivers a copy dated August 4, 1988.

In half an hour, Frankie arrives, carrying Curly's copy.

"Let us check the contents and identify the deaths of Thoma and Ann either in the general news or the obituary section," says the court official.

Surprisingly, there is nothing in the news about Thoma and Ann, but everyone notices an unexplained blank space in the newspaper. "That is where the obituary news was, in those blank spaces," Jaygust says.

"Josh must have erased them," Thalli says to the uproarious laughter of the robot man and Usha. Robot man laughs as if an earthquake shook the building, and his snot ejects out like rocket fuel. He extends his long arm and pulls on Thalli's hair, drags her over the table toward him, and wipes his nose on her Grateful Dead sari.

"Let go off me, you ape-man," Thalli says.

He lifts her 250-pound frame by her neck and deposits her in her seat using his long arm.

"If you aren't happy with the proof we verbally presented, we have additional proof for the death of Thoma and Ann," Noman says.

Everyone's ears perk up.

"We are all ears," Kuriyan says.

"This better not be another fiction," Ravanan says.

"We were able to invoke Thoma's spirit during a séance we conducted immediately after his death," Noman says, unsure if it would count as legitimate evidence.

"Did he bring Frankenstein with him?" Kuriyan asks. More laughter.

"Well, if you don't believe these facts, we think that Josh masterminded a scheme to kidnap our parents," Jaygust says. "We believe he asked a big Canadian man named *Monsoon Man* or *Death Man* to fetch them to Canada. They colluded to kill our parents secretly so that there would be no death records, robing us of our inheritance."

"Did Josh invite Bigfoot to kill Thoma and Ann?" both the lawyers ask.

"Unless we get official death certificates, we are not allowed, by law, to execute the will," Ravanan says. "The ball is in your court, folks! Bring the legal documents; don't come up with any cock-and-bull story again."

"The law explicitly states that if the death certificate cannot be produced in five years, the property will be disposed of. The government will give it away for public use or charity," Kuriyan says.

Ravanan consults the court official at this point and makes an announcement: "Let me extend you a fig leaf. If you can't produce death certificates in five years, you may approach the government at that time to see if they are willing to give you the property out of their good will. Mind you, the government is not obligated to do this."

The meeting concludes.

The Gang of Four meet at Curly's mansion.

"Did anyone get hold of death certificates?" Jaygust opens the meeting.

"I am praying," Noman says.

"I have made contact with someone from the Birth and Death Registry," Jaygust says. "They will issue us the certificates if we pay."

"How much?" Thalli asks.

"Twenty-five thousand rupees each," Jaygust says. "Consider the bribe as business investment. Mark up the sale price accordingly."

The Gang is puzzled at no one seeing Death Man, or rather, claiming not to have seen him. The very same people who swore that they had seen Death Man kidnapping the old couple and taking them to Heaven (Ann's destination) and Underworld (Thoma's destination) now claim they have no knowledge of it. It is as if there is a massive erasure of their memories.

"Josh erased their memories," Jaygust declares.

"My friend Rosa swears by the tomb of her dead father that she has no recollection of Death Man," Curly says. "She is the very one who swore by the tomb of her dead mother that Death Man carried our parents to outer space. I persuaded her to accompany me to Ravanan's office to attest to Thoma and Ann's death. She chickened out at the last moment, blaming me that I was making up stories."

"I think people's brains are shot," Thalli says.

The Gang retire to upstairs bedrooms just after dinner. Frankie and Curly sleep in the master bedroom, and the rest in bedrooms down the hallway. It is a hot summer day; the ceiling fans go full blast.

All of them dream that night, and it is the same dream.

Frankie is a light sleeper, having been diagnosed with insomnia. He tosses and turns in the bed. Snorings from Thalli and Noman ring aloud in the hallway. When Frankie gets convinced that all the rest drifted to sleep, he releases sleeping Curly's hand from his neck and gets up. He prowls up and down the hallway.

The Dream God descends to the mansion. The Gang is caught in the dream net that he casts. In the dream, the Gang produce death certificates and receive property deeds in a trial at Amballore Court.

The prowling Frankie stops dead in his tracks when he sees Jaygust emerging from his bedroom. Immediately after, Thalli, Noman, and Curly come out from their rooms. Frankie is about to take their toddy order when he realizes that something is amiss. They are sleepwalking!

Frankie, the insomniac, watches four somnambulists forming a line in the hallway and walking down the wide staircase as if under spell. It is obvious they are unaware of their surroundings. Frankie doesn't know that they are acting out a dream, and that too, the same dream.

"Order in the court! The trial of *Josh v. Gang of Four* is to commence," the judge orders.

The gathering includes close family members, friends, and curious public. Josh sits with Kuriyan Plamoottil, the plaintiff lawyer. Across from them sit the defendants—the Gang of Four. The defense doesn't have a lawyer; they are representing themselves.

The prosecution states the case.

"We accuse the defendants of altering Thoma's will to take possession of property deed," Kuriyan states.

Frankie turns on the stairway and the downstairs lights. The Gang proceed to the conference room and take seats around the table as if executing a preprogrammed computer command. Frankie notes that they look like robots, with no human expression. He follows them down the stairs and stays in the background.

Jaygust responds.

"Your Honor, even if things happened as the plaintiff states, Josh has no right to claim the property. He is older brother and is supposed to give us the entire property."

The judge intervenes. "Did you just say the plaintiff is right about the statements he made?"

Frankie can only hear Jaygust making the defense statement; he can't hear the judge. Only the dreamers can see the judge and hear him. He infers the presence of people in the dream via the reaction of the Gang members. He notices that during the dream sequence when the Gang don't speak, they concentrate on someone. Their eyes are focused on the same spot and move simultaneously, indicating the person of interest moves.

"Yes, Your Honor," Jaygust says. "We are here not to refute the plaintiff but to state that we deserve to get the entire property to ourselves."

There arise rumblings from the court crowd, as if a giant swarm of bees buzz. They can't believe the defense's ridiculous argument.

There is a telling absence of a defense lawyer, they figure. Such a lawyer wouldn't choose this too-late-now-to-correct line of argument.

"Case closed." Kuriyan whispers, turning to Josh. They give each other high-five.

"Tell the court how you altered the documents," the judge orders.

"Bingo!" Kuriyan whispered. The evidence he was seeking—objective evidence, not circumstantial—is about to pop out of Jaygust's mouth.

Jaygust states that he got janitor job at South Amballore Bank where he accessed the bank vault containing the will and changed its contents.

Frankie moves. He comes closer to the table—just in case they wake up and need something. He, by now, gathers that the Gang is addressing a judge. He infers that they are in a court of law and the case involves property dispute with Josh.

"Josh showed you generosity," Kuriyan says. "Show gratitude instead of greed. Thanks to Josh, you now have land to stand on."

"Josh did not give us enough," Jaygust says. "Don't look a gift horse in the mouth."

"Josh needs to give us more!" Jaygust's words are delivered at the top of his voice. He steps away from the defendant's stand and howls wildly.

While the audience is transfixed by Jaygust's howling, his nails elongate and become claws. Long hair sprouts out across his body. He gets enlarged fangs, and his eyes look like those of a wolf. He leaps in wide strides across the court floor and approaches the wall that has a mural of the nightly sky with a full moon. He stares at the full moon and starts howling.

Frankie can't believe his eyes. He sees clearly that Jaygust is undergoing a strange transformation; his hair suddenly grows across his body, he leaps across the floor and heads to a window and looking out of the window to the full moon, he starts howling.

The judge bangs his desk and declares, "Order in the court! Security, arrest him." Before security intervenes, Jaygust reaches Kuriyan and wraps his werewolf hands around his neck and starts strangling. His fangs bite into the lawyer's shoulder. Kuriyan pants and his lungs pump desperately to take in air.

Frankie follows Jaygust to the window. The werewolf turns around and notices Frankie staring at him; he wakes up from the dream. He grabs Frankie by the neck and starts strangling him. Frankie starts crying. This wakes up Gang members from their dream and they get a rude awakening: Jaygust is strangling Frankie. They run toward the two men and pull Frankie from Jaygust's grip. After a few moments, Jaygust regains his composure and normal appearance. He goes upstairs with the rest. They fall asleep. Frankie joins Curly in bed.

The dream resumes as soon as the Gang fall asleep.

The court convenes after a short break. The judge renders the verdict in favor of the defendants.

Josh's share of the land and the parental home are ordered distributed among the Gang of Four. Kuriyan feels that the court negligently overlooked the falsified document and passed erroneous judgment.

The Gang's cowardly backstabbing, instead of being vilified, is extolled by the guardian of the law, the Amballore Court. It is an instance of the law being steamrolled by the very entity that is supposed to uphold it. Josh decides not to appeal. "Let bygones be bygones." he says to his lawyer.

The Gang of Four meet at Amballore registry office to complete the property transaction and to celebrate. Their spouses and children accompany them. Lots of relatives join, forming a wide cross-section of Thoma's and Ann's descendants.

Chicken Little appears. He crows. "*Cock-a-doodle-doo! The sky is falling!*" The registrar is puzzled by the unannounced appearance of a wild rooster. The Gang members are seized by uproarious laughter.

They recognize the intruder as the same cock who'd predicted the sky's fall in 1975.

A podium is set up in the large meeting room adjoining the registry office. Jaygust climbs up to the podium on his one leg. He limps slowly but surely.

"*Cock-a-doodle-doo!*" he says as soon as he is on the stage. "The land and house fell from the sky! Folks, I got the windfall."

"Mirror, mirror, on the wall, who is the luckiest of them all?" he asks. "I am the luckiest of us all! My dear siblings, watch and suffer! I am the biggest winner amongst us."

He cockily hooks his thumbs in his expensive belt and looks around to make sure everyone is paying attention. He retrieves a comb and combs his hair.

"Don't forget that I got a university education—a free one. Without it, I would count the sheep every day. Ha-ha." The Gang joins in the laughter.

"I am employed by a bank, and I count money all day long, and this makes me feel rich—very rich!" The audience laughs.

The whole Amballore knows that Jaygust received his university degree after flunking multiple times. The university vice chancellor took pity on him and granted a mercy degree, if only to get rid of the oldest student in Amballore University.

"I gave Jaygust a mercy degree, just as a whore would give a mercy fuck to a client who couldn't afford her service," he says to his wife on convocation night. "That man doesn't deserve his degree. I fucking took pity on him."

The land registrar in the court is afraid Jaygust is going to narrate his life story. He shows no sign of concluding his speech. After all, he has a captive audience. The registrar calls security who takes him down from the podium, but he holds on to the platform rails, wiggles out of the security's hold, and climbs up to the podium to resume his speech.

"I believe in the falling skies. Who said it was hallucination that prompted Chicken Little to shout that the sky is falling? I saw the sky falling with my own eyes!" The audience roar with laughter.

The Gang members are in their respective bedrooms enacting the dream, and therefore insomniac Frankie is not privy to their facial expressions except that of his wife, who is sleeping nearby. He hears Jaygust's speech from the adjoining bedroom. He figures that the four siblings are no longer inside the court of law but instead in a social gathering where Jaygust is giving a speech.

The Gang members kneel and roll on the floor. All four adults growl like mad dogs and start biting the oriental carpet to pieces. The expensive carpet is torn into four pieces. They devour the pieces, one each.

Chicken Little's turn comes. "*Cock-a-doodle-doo! The sky is falling!*" he crows.

That is the last announcement he makes in his life because Jaygust catches him, carries him home, and makes chicken curry. He invites the Gang members. They eat the spicy curry over glasses of expensive French champagne.

Frankie realizes they are drinking champagne, judging from loud slurping sounds. He knows Jaygust and Noman did something to Josh, something harmful, but not sure what. He hears loud voices from the adjoining bedrooms. Curly is laughing like crazy but sleeping like a baby.

It is three in the morning. Curly's sleep turns normal. Frankie knows the party is over.

Thoma's and Ann's death certificates do not surface in spite of the best-efforts Gang of Four put to it.

The Amballore town authorities decide to hold the property in a trust until 1993, five years after Thoma and Ann's disappearance—legal timeframe for valid claims from the descendants. The town would qualify for permanent rights if proof of death doesn't materialize. In such case, it can dispose of the estate any way they please. If they show up, South Amballore Bank, the testator institution, gets the ownership title, and Ravanan executes the will to distribute the property among Thoma's children.

The trustee institution, Amballore Land Registry, builds a tall concrete wall around Thoma's property and declares it off limits to the public. The wall has a metallic front gate. A tamperproof lock keeps it securely closed.

When 1993 arrives, certificates are still a no-show. South Amballore Bank signs off on the property. Amballore town authorities take over and Thoma's children are declared as no inheritors.

Thoma is kicking in his grave, as Tim tells Rita: "Thoma's wish that his ungrateful children should be deprived of their inheritance came to fruition."

Thoma's long arms reach from beyond the grave and takes the Gang by their balls. This includes Thalli.

"I bet you have balls," Thoma told Thalli when he was alive.

The Gang's last option—appeal to the board to gift them with the estate—is turned down by the Town Board chairman because he felt that Amballore stands to gain by selling the property rather than giving it away. "But we are Thoma's children, his blood relations," Jaygust argues in vain.

ELEVEN

THE BURIAL

The year 2013 marks the 25th anniversary of Thoma's and Ann's grand departure to outer space. By this time, Gang of Four undergo some dramatic changes. Life has to go on.

Frankie surprises everyone by shaving off his moustache and beard in direct violation of Jaygust's fatwa-like embargo. The bearded man throws in the towel on getting clemency to clean up his face. He takes the law into his own hands.

Frankie doesn't give Curly advance notice on this monumental step.

The insomniac strolls his mansion in the middle of the night when Curly snores and the children sleep like babies. He plans on his insurgency on that long, sleepless night and decides on its solid execution. After a time- consuming shave, more like cleaning up a weed-infested yard, he joins Curly in bed, with earmuffs tightly wrapped around his head to cut off the snoring. He fits himself with dark eyeshades. He virtually becomes deaf and blind when he hits the sack at 1A.M.

"Get out of my bed, you bastard." Curly pulls out the knife from under the bed at around 8A.M. when she gets up and points it at Frankie. By that time, she had ripped off his earmuffs and eyeshade.

Frankie gets a rude awakening when his head gadgets get plucked off.

His first reaction upon hearing the loud screaming is Curly is snoring as usual. He turns around in the bed, but then something catches his eye. He rubs sleep off his eyes and realizes that his wife is about to stab him. Curly usually sleeps with a knife under her bed for protection, especially to fight off the nearby toddy shop's patrons who get the wrong idea and wander to her mansion at odd hours.

"Ma'am, it is me, your husband," Frankie pleads. He tries to dislodge his throat from her strong left-hand grip that nearly paralyzes him. She is straddling him.

She lowers the knife when she recognizes her husband's voice. She gazes at the apparent intruder and realizes that the son of a bitch has a dramatic change in appearance after a shave long overdue. She drops the knife.

"Next time you shave, you better let me know ahead of time, you ass!" Curly says.

"Yes, ma'am."

"You're lucky I didn't kill you." "Thank you, ma'am."

"You look like a criminal now," she says. "I want you to regrow your beard and moustache."

"Yes, ma'am."

Noman gives up on secular life one fine morning. He tells his wife that he is leaving her and their children because he got the call.

"You bloody weasel, are you out of your mind?" she says. "You can't walk out on married life, whatever the reason." Her fury is marked on her face with deep red color. She throws away the fish she is cleaning. Out through the kitchen door goes a boiling pot of rice. "To hell with your supper," she shrieks.

It takes some time for her fury to subside. The son-of-a-bitch is not changing his mind and he is in the doorway with a heartless demeanor, and she becomes disconsolate. She appeals to his common sense and basic human decency.

"How can you do this to me and our children?" She cries. The children hug her and cry with her, sending angry looks at Noman.

"I can't say 'no' to Jesus when he calls," Noman says with a stone face.

"Show some guts and say 'no' for the sake of your family," his wife pleads. "Prove to him you have balls." Her fury escalates.

Noman knows he can't prove to Jesus what his wife asks him to do. "Your Jesus won't forgive you for abandoning your wife and children," she says. "Why didn't you have the gall to walk out on me long ago before you saddled me with children?" She wipes her tears and consoles her crying children. She is despondent. "If so, I would have been relieved that I won't have to put up with your jackfruit face all these years." She weeps so desperately that she can't console her weeping children anymore.

"Praise the Lord," Noman says and walks out.

"Praise my ass," she calls out to him. That is the very last sentence she said to her husband, now her ex-husband.

He becomes an itinerary preacher speaking to sporadic crowds in Amballore about the message of Christ. From sunrise to sundown, people gather around him in scattered meadows in town. During monsoon rains, they hold open umbrellas to attend his sermon. They brave the long hot evenings of summer to be with him and receive his message. He goes from home to home, from the town center to the farmlands, and from crowd to crowd, preaching the message of love and sacrifice even though his wife believes he is the last man who could champion the noble virtues of Christianity.

Thalli's husband is called Cheapsmith for making cheap gold jewellery and selling them for high price. After marriage, he discovers that eight arms can sprout out of Thalli when she gets mad. Her notoriety as Bhadrakali makes terrorizing visit to him when he least expected.

It is one week after their marriage, at the end of the honeymoon in a cheap motel in Trichur, when he becomes witness to her paranormal ability. They get up in the morning of the last day of the honeymoon, have breakfast, and get ready to pack up their belongings and head out home.

"Pack my things while I shave," Cheapsmith says to his wife.

"Do it yourself; I ain't your servant," Thalli says. She is sleepy, tired, and groggy after spending a good part of the night killing bedbugs that crawled on her and her husband.

"You bitch, do what I say."

Thalli stands up, livid with anger. She lifts the chair she is sitting on and hurls at him, immediately realizing that the rattan chair is too light to cause serious harm. She walks to him with a threatening look, intent on smashing his face with her bare hands. Cheapsmith is seeing this side of his new wife for the first time and steps back. Then he sees it: she has eight arms! He picks up the chair as a shield against the approaching tigress. She pulls the chair with one arm and tosses it. Her seven other arms do no pulling; they just watch what her eighth arm is doing. The arm lifts him by his neck and holds him against the wall, half strangling him.

"Don't you talk to me like that ever again," she says, dropping him to the floor.

That is the last time Cheapsmith called his wife a *bitch.*

He starts making eight-armed goddesses in gold. This is quite a novelty, and the clients flock to his shop. He makes bracelets, necklaces, bangles, earrings, and numerous other items adorned with the eight-armed Bhadrakali.

One day, a customer comes to return the jewelry he bought. "Hey, you dirty crook, the goddess has only seven arms," he says to Cheapsmith and hurls the bracelet. "Where is the eighth arm? You charged me for eight arms, so return my money."

"Count again," Goldsmith says, throwing back the bracelet. His quick movement is fast like a magician's hand movement, and the customer is easily scammed to not take notice of Cheapsmith expertly exchanging the faulty one with a genuine one. The client counts again and realizes he made a mistake.

Jewelry swindling takes on an accelerated pace when seven arms reduce to six, six to five, and so on, until the goddess became two-armed. All along this process, the price remained the same—the price of an eight- armed goddess. He continues to defraud his clients by selling overpriced jewelry.

As she aged, Thalli's robust breasts droop to her belly button, having lost their elasticity. They stay with her like two old women pleading her to release them from their miserable existence. They appeal to her common sense to bury herself in a six-feet-deep pit so that they can rest in peace. As for her buttocks, they once protruded like voluminous jackfruits, sturdy and hostile like two enemy army soldiers. Now they are docile, their ruggedness depleted out of them, sagging toward Mother Earth like two lost children.

She continues to instill terror in Amballoreans because of her ongoing display of paranormal prowess. Some people think she indulges in black magic. As time goes on, she and her husband lead lonelier lives, isolated, disliked, and feared by Amballoreans.

Amballore citizens realize that Jaygust transforms to werewolf on full-moon nights. His two-story house is adjacent to Thoma's haunted property. During those nights, people gather around his house to see his silhouette against the translucent upstairs window curtain, cast by moonlight streaming through the opposite window.

Slowly, the curtain opens. They see a werewolf standing at the open window. The animal slowly emerges from the room to the balcony. It restlessly paces along the balcony, intermittently stopping and staring at something or someone across the yard in the adjacent property. Then they see the object of its fascination—Thoma's ghost is sitting in a wheelchair, staring back at the werewolf.

Thoma has been haunting his property ever since Death Man carried him to Underworld. The property remains unsold because of the ill reputation that it is haunted. A few years ago, the building structure collapses to the ground because of lack of regular maintenance. The town cleans up the debris, leaving behind just land. A prominent sign outside says that the property is for sale.

Lucky to Leave Alive
That is the name of the hotel Josh stays during his trip to Kerala from Canada in 2013. It is on the outskirts of Amballore and located along Lovers Lane.

The hotel lives up to its ominous name, Josh realizes. Lizards are freely roaming the bathroom and an occasional mouse or two scurrying across the kitchen floor. He feels lucky he doesn't encounter a snakecharmer in the living room, with a snake in full display of its fang. After a month's stay, he is going back to Canada. He sure feels lucky to leave alive.

"Sir, may I load your luggage?"

Josh jolts out of his thoughts. As he turns around, a uniformed cabdriver is standing there like an apparition in a horror movie. The man is dressed in khaki uniform and gray baseball hat. His lips crawl back to display yellow-stained teeth. He is smiling.

After checking out of the hotel, Josh has been waiting at the curbside to hail a taxi. His plan is to head out to the Cochin International Airport, some forty miles from Amballore. He is then to stay at the airport hotel before catching next day's flight to Dubai en route to Canada. Balan, the travel agent, assured him this is better than a last-minute race to the airport along a crowded freeway risking delay and possibly missing the flight.

Embroidered on the cabbie's hat is the name of the cab company, *We Race for You*. Not an inappropriate name, thinks Josh, though the cab races for money and not necessarily for the customer.

"Don't race for me; drive safe," Josh says.

"Yes, sir, we race for you," says the clueless cabbie.

The driver expertly steers the car to overtake the pedestrians, bicyclists, three-wheelers, and four-wheelers that crowd the road. There is total disarray all around, with vehicles and humans scrambling to take every little piece of the road ahead. They move in random directions like ants unable to make up their minds to move in straight lines. Josh feels the road scene is like a movie set managed by a mad director.

It is early evening. He watches the slanting rays of the setting sun settling in through the cab window. The swaying trees by the roadside seem to be saying goodbye to him. He is heading out of a tropical paradise to land of snow. A boring drive lasting three to four hours is ahead of him.

He falls asleep despite the jittery movements of the car caught in numerous potholes. When he wakes up, he is alone in the cab. It is pitch-dark. The cab is in the middle of nowhere. The driver has vanished. A cacophony of nocturnal sounds from crickets and tree frogs gives him an eerie feeling. He fishes out cell phone from the pocket, only to realize it is out of range. Gradually it dawns on him that he is in some remote wilderness, far from the freeway, far from civilization.

Where is the driver?

From the backseat he gazed at the dashboard and is alarmed to see the key missing. Did the driver abandon him?

Then again, maybe not. In his mind's eye Josh starts seeing eerie scenes of the driver intercepted by a three-headed police officer who hijacks the vehicle and drives it to a jungle where he hands the driver to a gang of cannibals with protruding tummies, pierced noses, and fiery eyes. The savages boil the cabbie in coconut oil as part of their primitive ritual of human sacrifice. They dance around the boiling pot in aboriginal rhythmic steps in tune with a prehistoric song without script, more like jackals howling. Their drumbeats reverberate in the still air of the night, waking snoring men and women miles away.

Josh expects them to drop in any time, to capture him and repeat the nightmarish ritual. He is next on their plate.

He gets out of the cab, takes a leak, and zips up. Someone taps on his shoulder. He screams out loud and turns around.

"Sir, I am back!" says the cabby respectfully hunching over, ready to serve.

"Where were you, dick-head?" Josh scream, staring closely at the cabby to make sure that he is not a cannibal in disguise. "I took a break, sir," the cabby apologizes.

He confirms that aliens or three-headed policeman did not abduct him. He was not fried in coconut oil either. He took a detour from the highway to purchase toddy.

"I didn't want to wake you up, sir; you were sound asleep," he says. "I know a house nearby selling bootlegged alcohol."

"You shouldn't have left me alone in the wilderness," Josh says.

"I bought two bottles, sir," the highway butler says. "One for you and one for me." He dishes out gleaming bottles of white palm wine.

"Don't drink; you're the driver," Josh says. "Don't forget you have to drive forty miles tonight."

"That will be twenty miles, sir; we already crossed twenty," he says. "Don't worry, sir. I won't get drunk. I promise in the name of my deceased father."

He reveals that his father was a cabdriver and that he was killed while driving drunk a few years ago.

"Does it run in the family?" Josh asks.

"My father was in the accident when he drove a Canadian Malayali to the same airport you're going to, sir," he says. He finishes half the bottle in a long draught. "The passenger also was killed."

Josh shudders at the thoughtless revelation the stupid driver made and hope not to meet with the same fate.

"Don't you dare kill me."

"Rest assured, sir! I'll drop you off alive at the airport," the dead cabby's son says.

They hop back inside the car, Josh taking the backseat. The driver drains the rest of the toddy in another long swallow.

"I see you're a natural in toddy drinking," Josh says. "It must come as easy as breathing."

"No; it comes to me as easy as peeing, sir," the cabbie corrects. He starts the car.

That is when it happened.

The driver is about to change gear to put the cab in motion. Josh is wide awake to see what is happening.

Suddenly the driver's door opens wide, and an invisible force pulls the cabbie, as evidenced by the horror-stricken cabbie screaming, and ejecting out of the car involuntarily. The force that pulled him out is brutal enough to strip the seatbelt. It is so ferocious that the cabbie is airborne like a rocket they send from Thiruvanathapuram space station.

The invisible force enters the car. The driver's door closes in a snap, the gear shifts, and the car is in motion.

"Who are you?" Josh asks. No answer.

The driver drives over the twists and turns of the rugged country road.

Then it strikes Josh—the car doesn't have headlights on! The lunatic is driving in pitch-darkness.

"Turn on the headlights," Josh says.

The beast continues to drive in the dark. Being driven by an invisible driver, It is a driverless car for all practical purposes. Josh is the only visible human inside. Gradually the driver starts taking shape. The moonlight reveals a baseball hat materializing over the driver's seat. Next, a khaki shirt appears underneath the hat. There is no human body to wear the hat or the shirt.

The car approaches the freeway. Instead of turning toward the airport, it turns in the opposite direction, toward Amballore.

"Circle the car around and head to the airport," Josh orders.

Neither the hat nor the shirt responds. The cab continues its course to Amballore. Josh risks being delayed or missing the flight. He is losing valuable time. He tries to reason with the invisible driver, but the pleadings fall on deaf ears.

A few minutes down the freeway, a body materializes on the driver's seat. The hat and the shirt fit the body perfectly. A live person or a live something is at the wheel. After taking the Amballore exit, the cab drives painfully slow down the interior roads as if in a sightseeing tour. It then stops at a property. Josh didn't need introduction to the property; it is the same he bought for the family years ago.

"Sir, this is your destination."

At last, the man is talking! Josh is sure he heard that voice before. Where did he hear it?

The cabbie turns around. Josh eagerly gazes at the mysterious driver, but there is no one there; the baseball hat stares at him.

Josh gets out and reviews the property; it is heavily fortified. Tall walls surround it. Its heavy-duty metallic gate is kept locked, blocking access to the public. A "For Sale" sign is posted prominently on the front wall. He is aware that Thoma haunted the property, as reported by many, including the patrons of Judas Toddy Club. This notoriety blocks all the attempts at its sale. The Amballore Estate Board put it on the market in 1993, when the five-year grace period to produce Thoma and Ann's death certificates lapsed.

There is only land inside—the ancestral home has vanished. As for the outhouse, there is no trace of it either. The breed of outhouse is becoming extinct, falling under the category of endangered species, Josh thinks.

Modern Kerala houses has attached bathrooms.

He gazes at the property through the black metal grills of the front gate. A lush yard filled with numerous tropical plants is visible in the moonlight. The plantain leaves sway and flutter in the breeze. The majestic coconut palms appear to be beckoning him with their broad fronds as if they are gigantic banners according him a riotous welcome.

While he is thus studying the property, the heavy-duty lock clicks open and the gate swings inward as if acted upon by an invisible sentry. Josh lets himself in. The air in the yard has a peculiar brownish-orange tint, and it contrasts with the transparent air outside. The yard is awash with numerous shadows of palm leaves cast by the full moon. They move erratically as if in a shadow play, as if narrating the family story of long past.

He walks to the tall coconut palm from whose trunk Thoma shook off his ungrateful son, Jaygust, twenty-nine years ago, plunging him into the outhouse. The tree stands there mysteriously, as if waiting for Josh. It is as majestic as ever, defeating the flow of time, minimally weather-beaten, hosting not even a single wrinkle.

It stays in the yard in profound silence, probably waiting for another bastard (Jaygust, born out of wedlock, is the first bastard) to climb it so that another Thoma can shake him off. Albeit a tree of no words, it appears to know and say a lot more things than it has been given credit for. Josh caresses the legendary palm and then embraces it. It sways as if reciprocating the hug. Its trembling branches welcome Josh with open arms.

Suddenly, a windstorm blows from the nearby graveyard, shaking the trees. The untamed wind picks up momentum, howling like a band of jackals, its witheringly ferocious force shaking the palm's sweeping leaves.

The tree trunk starts oscillating. The coyotes in the distance yelp savagely, helplessly. The dogs in the street bark and run away, tails tucked between legs, the cats meow angrily. The growling skies send thunder and lightning. Black clouds resembling huge festival umbrellas gather over the yard, ready for a tumultuous downpour. The nightingale, the bird of the night, perches on the tall areca nut tree. Mother Nature waits in anguished anticipation of something.

It rains with raging madness.

The rain stops after some time. At that very moment, Josh sees someone descending from the top of the palm. He is not climbing down the tree; he is floating and descending as if in a parachute.

"Josh," calls out the parachuting man. "Don't be afraid. This is me, your father."

He lands. The wind stops. The turbulence in and around the yard is subdued and tranquility returns. Josh looks at the mysterious presence and recognizes him. He unmistakably identifies his father in the full moonlight. Thoma has a headful of hair and deep wrinkles on his face, and he wears glasses. His lips are dark—persistent beedi smoking made them so. A wide belt is strapped around his waist. Attached to the belt is a toddy bottle.

"I am here to be buried," says the ghost.

"But you are dead and gone!" Josh says. "You can't be buried."

"I didn't get a proper burial when I left this world," Thoma says. "I want to be buried under this coconut palm by you."

This surreal request made Josh uncomfortable. He has never been an undertaker, never cremated a body, never buried it either.

"But you are a spirit, you have been dead for years. You can't be entombed."

"I am as real as I appear to you, my son."

"A burial just a short time before my flight? I am already late." "Your flight can wait," Thoma says. "Since you asked, let me tell you why it is you who should bury me."

Thoma unhooks the toddy bottle from his belt and swigs multiple gulps and continues. "It was you who saved me and family from starvation. Death would have knocked at our door if you hadn't stepped in with your rescue mission from Canada. You gave us a second chance. You renewed our lease on life. You are my real landlord, not Chettiar."

Josh notes that Thoma is very chatty, just as he has always been when drunk. He suspects that Thoma makes toddy at the top of the palm. This explains his descent from its top with a bottle strapped to his waist.

"Are you sure you are not drunk?" Josh asks. He is still incredulous at the outlandish request from his father.

"Death Man kidnapped me in 1988. You sure know that. He abducted me and Ann. He took out the white sack in his black-and-white gown's right pocket and dropped her at heaven's doorstep. I stayed in the black sack in his left pocket and watched the delivery.

"Next, he carried me to Underworld, dropped me there and left. A huge pyre was burning there, which would have incinerated an elephant instantly. The cremationist looked at me, shook his head, and said, 'I refuse to cremate you.' He walked away.

"I stayed there staring at the blazing inferno, being denied entry. I told myself that I am an eternal homeless guy; even the hell's fire is refusing to take me in."

The narration intrigues Josh despite the bizarre circumstances he presently finds himself in. Thoma has an intriguing style of narration. Josh especially likes the depiction of his soul not having a home, just like his body did not have a proper home while living in Mannuthy rental. Thoma is an eternal tenant.

"The undertaker came back, taking pity on my plight. He had a change of heart.

'OK, I am going to take a chance with you,' he said. 'I will throw you in the fire. Mind you, it will only give you minor burns. You are made of the stuff that doesn't die.' *Ha-Ha-Ha*, he laughed.

'How so?' I asked him.

'You are one of a kind, Thoma! You do not conform to the Laws of Nature,' he laughed again.

'I don't want to go back to earth; Incinerate me and be done with it,' I pleaded.

"He tossed me to the fire. As he said, I only got minor burns, I didn't die. Therefore, he decided to send me back to earth. He endowed me with supernatural powers to deal with my second life on earth.

'You can't die. If you wish to do so, the only person who can do it is your son Josh,' he said while pulling me out of the fire.

'How so?'

'Because he gave you a life you did not deserve; only he can take it back.'

"He then gave me some advice on my forthcoming stay on earth. 'While on earth, be careful of the mortals: they have short memories, they are thankless, they will bury you alive, don't trust them.' 'You are telling me!' I replied.

"He then gave me power over the humans.

'I give you power to change past events. But use it wisely.'

"I was given special power to change previous events—imagine that!

I could change the past to affect the present and future. It was like I am getting bestowed with Time Travel gift. I was almost like God. I was then sent back to earth.

"As I was approaching earth, I felt a powerful pull and was drawn into Curly's home. Gang of Four had assembled there, and they were conducting a prayer séance to communicate with me to confirm I was dead. Once confirmed of my death, they could claim their inheritance. I gave those four bastards a scary night they would never forget. I all but killed them."

The floating clouds briefly eclipse the moonlight, but they clear.

Thoma continues. "I taught the greedy bunch a lesson. I used my powers to erase the obituary section of *Amballore Times* that had narrated Ann's and my demise. I also erased the memories of Amballoreans who had witnessed our kidnappings by Death Man."

Now Josh knows the reason behind the inexplicable absence of Thoma's and Ann's obituaries in *Amballore Times*. This intrigued the probate lawyers and the court official who met after the death to execute the will.

Josh was also aware of another strange happening at that time. Per the conversation he had with Tim and Rita, the witnesses denied any knowledge of Death Man's abduction of the elderly couple. Even though there was evidence in the form of a massive number of burnt candles on the ground in and around Thoma's yard, no one remembered Death Man kidnapped Thoma and Ann.

Thoma continued after patting the coconut palm. "The last thing Gang of Four deserved was the inheritance. I made sure all the roads leading to that eventuality were closed.

"I am haunting this place and leading a happy life." He looks at the full moon for a moment and continues. "I could have contacted you and brought you here earlier to release me from this bondage. But I didn't, because I confess that I enjoy my new-found life which comes with supernatural powers. Living without care is something I couldn't have in my previous life. Now it has become a reality.

Thoma takes another swig from the bottle and continues.

"Can you imagine, Josh? It takes death to appreciate life and to live it better. I know it because I went through the motions." Thoma smiles.

"Now it is time to go, I've had enough fun. Therefore, I am making an entreaty to you, my dear Josh, to release me from the life you gave me.

Please bury me under this coconut palm, which is my beloved friend. Only you can do this—only you!"

The bizarre request to bury Thoma terrifies Josh, because Thoma is alive—well, sort of.

"If you don't release me from this bondage, I'll be stranded in Kerala," Thoma says. "Then I am doomed to haunt this yard forever."

Suddenly, the palm tree starts shaking and swirling. A ditch materializes underneath the tree and around it. An invisible gravedigger keeps making the ditch deeper and deeper until it reaches six feet deep. The dug-up dirt is scattered around the tree in a heap. The ditch has been meticulously made to ensure the tree does not collapse. The roots are intact. Thoma hugs Josh, bids him goodbye, and jumps into the grave.

"All you have to do is fill in the grave," Thoma's voice comes from underground.

Josh now sees something equally amazing—a shovel descends toward him from the top of the palm. It lands by his feet.

Thoma's voice once more ascends from the grave. "When you complete your task, I can at last rest in peace. All these years I had dreams of you coming here to release me from my bondage, my dear Josh! Now, go ahead and do it! After that, go back to Canada. Go there and prosper. May only good things happen to you."

Josh tears up at his old man's words. He can't resist the sobs that take root in the belly. He says a final goodbye to his father and buries him. He steps back and says a prayer:

Oh skies, lead him to a place of rest Bright as day to ride out gloom Beckon him to a place of tranquility Where his soul can rest in peace Thoma's voice comes from underground. "Josh, I was doomed to raise a family whose members fought like archenemies, like India and Pakistan. You made a difference by building an oasis in the scorching desert. Remember, Ann and I will never forget what you did for us. We are eternally grateful to you."

Those are the last words from Josh's father to him, words of gratitude. Josh is content to hear them from his old man. Thoma's acknowledgment is good enough for him. Those are the only words of gratitude I need to hear; Josh tells himself.

Josh heads toward the waiting cab. Just before getting into the cab, he gazes at the property for the last time. His eyes involuntarily dart to the second-floor window of the nearby home. Against the moonlight streaming through the window, Josh sees an unmistakable silhouette which moves out of his view as soon as he gazes at it.

The man behind the silhouette, Jaygust, has been watching the entire supernatural encounter between Thoma and Josh unbeknown to them, Josh is convinced.

As Josh turns around, there is another quick movement at the window.

He looks up again. This time, there is a werewolf standing in Jaygust's place, and it is staring at Josh.

The animal turns around, stares at the full moon, opens its mouth, and howls.

TWELVE

SEPTEMBER
FULL MOON MASSACRE

"Hurry up and head to the airport," Josh says to the cab driver. The invisible cabbie eases the cab into the road and is headed to the highway. Instead of taking the freeway entrance ramp to the airport, he heads in the opposite direction to Mannuthy.

"To the airport, you hear?" Josh screams.

The cabby ignores the request and goes beyond the speed limit and suddenly stops in the middle of the highway. Honking cars zip by; angry faces stare at Josh and the baseball hat. A red Corvette speeding behind applies the brake at the last moment, avoiding a fatal collision.

"Up yours, you ass," the Corvette says while careening dangerously close.

"Up yours too, you red bastard," the invisible cabbie says.

Corvette peeks at the cab driver, only to see no one. The bearded man is puzzled and even panicked and takes off in high acceleration. Cabbie's window slides down, baseball hat eases out of the cab and chases the red car. Other drivers crane their necks out to see the race between the Corvette and the hat. The hat overtakes the Corvette, turns around and comes hurtling toward it and hits the windshield. The corvette applies brakes and stops dead in the road. The hat steers itself and enters the Corvett through open window.

"Don't you ever call me an ass," the hat says, slips out, and heads to the cab.

The invisible cabbie adjusts the hat and continues to sail along the highway. Josh notices an old woman walking across the highway. She doesn't wait for the vehicles to pass before crossing the lanes and gets dangerously close to the speeding cars. Angry drivers honk the horns and steer around her. She wears a chatta and mundu and holds a rosary and prays. The cabbie stops the cab and opens the door. She enters the car as if it is pre-planned. She takes seat near Josh. The cab moves.

Josh gazes at the woman and realizes she is a very old woman with silver hair, probably nearing one hundred years. He thinks he has seen her before somewhere. He peers at her closely and recognition hits him like lightning. It is Ann, his mother!

The surreal night has not exhausted its supernatural visions yet, Josh thinks.

"How nice to see you, Josh!" Ann hugs Josh, shedding tears of happiness.

"Same here, Mother," Josh says. "Just what do you think you're doing crossing the highway? You could get run over!" He kisses her old wrinkly face.

"They can't kill a ghost, ha-ha-ha!" Ann laughs hilariously.

The cabdriver now materializes. His head emerges first, then a body fills the T-shirt, and the hat rests on his head. He turns around. He has a lizard face and blazing eyes.

He is Monsoon Man! Now Josh knows why he thought he recognized his voice earlier in the night.

"I am taking you both to your Mannuthy rental," says Monsoon Man. "Feel free to thank me."

"I brought you a gift." She says to Josh and retrieves something from inside her chatta.

Josh turns on the back light and examines Ann's gift, which is wrapped in a plantain leaf. He opens the package. Inside is a very old newspaper made yellow by the passage of time. In the dim light, Josh struggles to read. It is copy of *Amballore Times* dated August 4, 1988—the day after the momentous arrival of Death Man who hauled off Thoma and Ann. He reads the obituary of his parents:

> *Amballore was seized by an extraordinary event just yesterday. The respected members of Amballore citizenry, Thoma and Ann, were abducted by Death Man who hauled them beyond the solar system to remote corner of the universe. The spectators described the strange-looking abductor as a breed between lizard and Underworld demon. During the encounter between him and the old couple, he grew to the size of the sky and beyond, his head reportedly reaching the planet Neptune.*

Amballore Times takes this moment to express our sorrow at the disappearance of the couple. May their souls rest in peace.

Those words were invisible ever since Thoma made his way back to earth from Underworld. Josh remembers Tim sending him *Amballore Times* at that time to Canada but was perplexed not to find his parents' obituary.

Josh realizes that earlier in the night he buried the power that made such a supernatural feat possible, which led to the reappearance of the news.

Monsoon Man stops in the street in front of the Mannuthy rental home. It is early morning. Josh's heart skips a beat at seeing the old rental, a warehouse of his youth's memories. It is standing in the same old spot and is seemingly unruffled by the passage of time.

"Here you are, have fun!" he says and cuts off the engine.

Ann and Josh cross the street and enter the rental's front yard. The house stands there as if expecting them. It tells them that its troubled past is distant memory. There is a small garden in the yard, product of the years after they left. Lilacs flutter in the soft morning breeze to welcome the ancient tenants.

An old woman watches them from the porch of the neighboring rental.

She is comfortably seated in a wheelchair. She waves a hand fan back and forth to drive the mosquitoes away. She wears a white cotton sari. There are wavy yellow lines on her wrinkled forehead. Josh estimates her age as hundred years.

"Bhavany, is that you?" Ann says when they get closer to the woman.

She does not hear. "What did you say?" She cups her ears and half stands up with a cane. She is a hunchback. Advanced Parkinson's disease makes her tremor.

"Bhavany, is that you?" Josh repeats loudly.

The woman stares at them, confused. She then almost jumps from where she stands. Her face is suddenly lit with recognition.

"Oh my god!" Bhavany says in quivering voice. "Is that you, Ann?"

Bhavany, her beloved neighbor in Mannuthy, a witness to her dismal life with its many-sided anguishes, is standing there in person! She was her and family's comforter, always by her side at moments of seemingly everlasting trials.

"I thought you died." Bhavany gazes at Ann in disbelief.

Ann does not answer; instead, she sheds her broad smile. Bhavany drops her fan and walks a few steps toward the visitors, leaning heavily on the cane. The two women hug each other.

Bhavany's trembling arm refuse to let Ann go. "Who is this man with you?"

"Don't you remember me? I'm Josh."

He hugs Bhavany. She is too weak to stand on her own. Josh wraps her inside his arms and seats her in the wheelchair. He retrieves her fan from the floor, and hands it to her.

It is thirty-eight years since they left Mannuthy. Josh is surprised that Bhavany is still living there. Her children, two daughters, got married and left long ago. Her husband, Kumaran, died a few years ago. She lives alone, with a maid to help her out. She is grandmother to five children.

"How I missed you all these years!" she says.

Her lonely life is in sharp contrast to the noise-ridden life of the past when she and Ann were neighbors, each saddled with husband and children. Bhavany is ten years younger than Ann, making her eighty-seven now but she looks older. Josh notes that her snow-white hair is in sharp contrast to the cascade of cloud-dark hair that bristled with life, youth, and vibrancy once upon a time. She was beautiful like the red roses she watered in her yard, but now she is anything but.

"It's nice to be back," Ann says. "This is where I belong." She has always felt Mannuthy is where her destiny took her and where she is ultimately supposed to be.

"Seeing you is like going back to the old days," Bhavany says. Ann strokes Bhavany's silver hair. "I couldn't agree more."

Josh gets hold of the landlord in the meantime. He is a grandson of Chettiar. He opens the door to their old rental. It has no tenants now.

Ann and Josh walk across Bhavany's courtyard into the old rental. Josh wheels Bhavany with them. The yard and the surroundings are in the same shape and form as they were long ago. Ann stands in front of the home, staring at it with unbelieving eyes, overcome by emotions at seeing her past sitting there. The house embodies the story of her youth, she knows.

They get inside. There is an overpowering silence. Here is a home whose walls could write a long, sad novel about her family, but it stands there silently, too dumbfounded at seeing Ann, its unforgettable tenant. Here is a home whose interior echoed with laughter, weeping, and screaming once upon a time but now stands still.

The porch has a flower-print curtain. Once upon a time, it did not have a fabric curtain but instead a palm-leaf curtain at night, which came down in the morning. Her sons and husband slept on the porch and the girls with her inside the interior bedroom. Thoma's nonstop coughing used to wake up the boys and the girls. They did their school homework under streetlamps just outside the porch. It is where Kumaran used to give free haircuts to her children.

She enters the bedroom. The room was used as a prayer room as well. She kneels and prays silently to the walls where a rosary hung long ago. This is the room where she woke up in the middle of the night to pray, pouring out her heart and soul to God, haggling with him over the trials sent her way, and imploring him to set her free from despair. This is where the family met to read Kareena's letters. This is where they sought shelter from the monsoon rains that leaked into the house. This is where her beautiful daughter Rafeena was murdered and her other daughter, Wilma, disappeared from. The attic is just above the bedroom. Thoma annexed it illegally to make room for his growing family, triggering a fight with the landlord. She recaptures the memories and absorbs the emotions unleashed by them.

She passes though the bedroom and gets in the kitchen. It is white-washed and ready to rent. Once upon a time, its walls were anything but white; the smoke from the clay oven turned the walls black. She bends down and peers in the oven. She used to spend untold hours there blowing into the oven, smoke hovered around her, and then her incessant blowing would suddenly light up the firewood she'd collected from the nearby rubber plantation. She softly blows into the unresponsive oven for old times' sake.

She gazes at the kitchen door that once hosted a sizable hole. A stray dog used to let itself in through the hole and eat their dinner occasionally, leaving the family hungry. Now the door looks as good as new.

"How I hated that dog!" Josh says. Ann smiles

Ann looks around the kitchen walls and focuses on its small window.

She is overcome with emotions and starts sobbing. She is reminded of the blackest of the black days in that kitchen, when Chettiar raped her in the presence of Subashini. Through her sobbing, she declares to the whole world that she was once attacked in her own kitchen, even though the world already knew. She tells the kitchen walls of the horrific incident, even though they saw it happen with their own eyes.

She steps out of the kitchen into the backyard. The mango tree is still there. It is stirring in the breeze, a silent witness to her past. A few unripe mangoes hang from its branches. She approaches the tree and kisses it fondly. A mother hen tends to her little chicks, feeding them worms she collected. She remembers she used to feed their ancestors curry and rice. A few ducks walk by, quacking and forming a line as if in a backyard parade in celebration of Ann's arrival.

She turns around and approaches the water well that once provided water for her cooking. She and her daughters used a bucket to bail water from it. The iron pulley is now rusted. The well looks the same, except its brick walls host graffiti from a wandering artist. "Jesus Saves," the writing says. For old times' sake, Ann drops the bucket, bails out water, and drinks few sips. She simultaneously drinks in the memories that overpower her.

She walks around and enters the porch again. She stares at the spot where Josh stood just before he took off for Canada in 1975. "Josh, darling, do you remember this spot?" she asks. He doesn't. "Your very last footsteps in this house are imprinted on this spot, but they are also the very first footsteps of your dream journey to Canada. These footsteps mark our family's liberation."

She steps into the invisible footsteps, now lost to the pages of history and forgotten. "You did not come back to this house after you left," she weeps. "I came here today to tell you that the family owes our lives to you. I know it in my heart; I feel it in my guts. I can't forget it ever because I keep remembering it."

Josh leans forward and wipes Ann's tears.

Bhavany's servant girl brings a tray with tea and jackfruit.

"No one stayed long at your rental after you left," Bhavany says. "The house has been empty ever since two renters left."

"How come?" Josh asks.

"Chettiar disappeared the day you left Mannuthy. His eldest son, Ravi, took over the family business and became the new landlord. Within two days after you left, he rented the house to a new tenant, a middle-aged couple with a teenage daughter. The very first day they moved in, they complained about a horrible stench. Even we got a whiff. They left the same day they moved in; they couldn't take it."

Josh remembers the letter from Mannuthy he received in Canada at the time his family moved out, detailing the bizarre events of their last night there. Thoma hung Chettiar's head from the attic ceiling that night. The rotting head explains the stench.

Bhavany eats a piece of jackfruit and continues. "The new landlord could not locate the source of the stench. He said the smell was inside the house and speculated it was coming from the walls. As time went on, the smell went down, and after a few months it was completely gone. Ravi was able to rent it to another family exactly one year after you left."

Monsoon Man left the car on to let the air conditioning cool the interior. The lizard-faced man sitting in the driver's seat and snoring loudly. Little kids gather around the cab and giggle.

"The second family who moved in was a family with ten children, just like your family. Kumaran and I welcomed the new family as if they were your family."

Josh approaches Bhavany, takes her hand fan, and wave it for her. "Everything seemed normal in the beginning. We expected them to stay for a long time. But soon, we knew it was just calm before the storm."

"What happened?" Ann asks.

"Kumaran and I heard loud weeping from our new neighbors and jumped out of our bed to investigate. It was early morning. We lit our kerosene lamps and got out. We learned that their eighth child, a girl, was missing. Immediately we called police. The police search team combed the neighborhood and at last found her—hanging under Mannuthy Municipal Bridge, with her long hair wrapped around bridge's metallic beam. Police confirmed it was not a suicide; she had been strangled before the culprit hung her by hair."

Bhavany chews on betel leaf pasted with white lime. "You left during September of 1975," she says, spitting out betel's red liquid. "The girl died on the anniversary of your departure."

Josh is struck by the uncanny resemblance of the girl to his sister.

Thalli was twenty-one on the day the girl was murdered. Does it mean that she would have been murdered if the family didn't move out? The family lost Rafeena and Wilma, the former a murder victim and the latter a kidnap victim. The disasters happened when each turned twenty-one. What is it about twenty-one-year-old women that fascinates the apparent serial murderer? Josh wonders.

"The family left after the tragedy; they thought the house was haunted," Bhavany says. She finishes her breakfast. "The news of the tragedy spread far and wide. The landlord has been unable to get tenants ever since."

"Mannuthy citizens continue to witness a bizarre murder on the anniversary of your departure, in September full moons.

"The first is the girl's murder in 1976, as I just narrated. From 1977 onward, a twenty-one-year-old woman is randomly chosen from this town and strangled to death and hung under the bridge. It is known as *September full moon massacre.*

"*The next murder happens* tonight which is the 37th anniversary of the first murder."

That is the end of Bhavany's story. Josh wheels her back to her house.

When they leave, their unforgettable neighbor is sitting in the wheelchair, her feet resting on a footrest. They wave goodbye. Ann and Josh see tears in her eyes. She knows that she would never see her neighbors ever again.

The two supernatural encounters, one involving his father and other his mother, effectively put a stop to Josh's scheduled flight to Canada. A new task suddenly shows up on his list. It is an undertaking he did not anticipate but now shows up with extreme urgency, something that screams for his full attention. Canada can wait, he decides.

The day he and Ann met with Bhavany hosted the night of the full moon of September. Tonight, an unlucky twenty-one-year-old Mannuthy woman will be murdered and hung under Mannuthy bridge. He could stop it if he hurries.

He heads out to the offices of *Mannuthy Chronicles*, the local newspaper. The friendly receptionist fetches him past editions of September full moons. The murder is on its front page in bold letters year after year.

The news says that the annual horror show defies attempts at its unraveling, intrigues the investigators, and forces them to throw in the towel. "Every attempt to get to the bottom of the mystery has proven futile," The paper says. "Investigative journalists of every stripe are at their wits' end."

Josh meets the senior editor who covered the news over the years. He is a silver-haired old man who started his career as a young twenty-five- year-old some forty years ago. He has a thick white moustache. Baldness claims most of the real estate on his head. A thin strip of snow-white hair goes around the back and the sides of his head, spelling out the letter *U*. Raghavan Menon sits in his dusty office, surrounded by numerous past editions of *Mannuthy Chronicles,* and peers at Josh through his rimless glasses.

"It'll happen tonight!" he says excitedly. "Our crew will take up position under the bridge."

"Who brings the body and hangs it?" Josh asks.

Menon pulls out a packet of cigarettes, lights up one, and puffs. "This is American cigarette; my son brought it on his last trip, outfoxing the customs," he winks. "My other son from Canada brings me Canadian beer bribing the customs with a few bottles. Ha-Ha-Ha!" He sends thoughtful circles of smoke toward the fluorescent lamp hanging above, making the mosquitos scramble. "Here, have a cigarette," he offers.

Josh declines.

"Now, back to your question," Raghavan says. "No one brings the body. That is the problem. While our press crew, municipal officials, and police force assemble under the bridge holding their breath in nerve-wracking anticipation, the young woman's body suddenly appears right in front of our eyes when the clock strikes two in the morning."

"Impossible," Josh says. "A dead body can't fly and appear as if from nowhere."

"Ha-Ha-Ha," he laughs loud enough to be heard around the building. "I like your description—a flying dead body." He leans back on his chair, looking up and studying the ceiling. "The body, just prior to the clock striking two, is seen floating in the air and arriving under the bridge. The crowd makes room to let it pass. It doesn't arrive by flying; it floats. Ha-Ha- Ha."

"Dead body doesn't move by itself," Josh says. "Isn't it carried by someone?"

"Yes, yes, yes, yes," said Raghavan, stopping his impulse to send unending stream of *yeses*. "Yes sir! I believe the body is carried by the invisible murderer who has fascination for bridges." He then pulls out his desk drawer and retrieves a toddy bottle, extending it to Josh. "Don't decline this; it is a sign of our hospitality," the editor says.

Josh didn't decline.

"Josh, my friend—can I call you, *my friend*?" "If you insist."

"My friend, if you are in investigative journalism, you will become a drunk," the editor says, sipping toddy. "Without toddy, I'm nothing.

Journalism is a pain in the neck; investigative journalism is a pain in the butt. I had a headful of hair once, but the stress of the job ate its way into making me a bald man."

"Please continue." Josh is eager to get to the bottom of the story. "Ah yes! As I said, the dead body appears exactly at two, like clockwork. The girl has long hair, always, always! The invisible man hangs her body under the bridge with her long hair wrapped around the beam, while we are gripped by suspense and horror. Here is a collection of pictures from over the years." He pulls out a package from the drawer.

Josh gazes at the photos. All the women have long hair like Rapunzel, like Thalli.

"They are all freshly killed women and look as good as alive. They are young and beautiful—not like me, an old hag." He laughs.

Josh examines the bridge and confirms it is the same bridge where Thalli butchered Chettiar.

"What do the police do while the body is hung?" Josh asks. "Do they arrest the invisible hangman?"

"Ha-Ha-Ha," the editor undergoes another laughing fit. "I like the way you put it, my friend, *arresting the invisible hangman.* As a matter of fact, police tried to arrest the intruder. Since he could not see the hangman, he guessed where his hands would be and fastened the handcuffs around them. But the device fell off to the ground; he had arrested the thin air. Ha-Ha- Ha!"

"What happened then?"

The editor puffs out more thoughtful smoke rings.

"As the handcuffs hit the ground, the hangman threw the police up in the air. All we could see was the policeman spontaneously getting airborne, hinting at an invisible somebody who did the throwing. His scream died down in a few seconds since he landed in the river." Raghaven retrieves a comb from his pocket and combs his U-shaped strip of hair. "The police learned their lesson that day. Ever since, the massive number of people assembled on the riverbanks and under the bridge on the September full moon nights did not interfere with the invisible murderer's operation. 'Leave him alone if you love your life' is what the police says to the public." He laughs, baring his smoke-stained teeth.

"I love American cigarettes. Don't forget I love Canadian beer too," the editor says while wrapping up the interview.

Josh knows he must visit Mannuthy rental once again. He has something to do there, something so important that he would lose peace of mind if he didn't. He rents a hotel room in Mannuthy, reschedules his flight, hires a taxi, and heads to his destination.

Monsoon Man parks in the street and is to remain inside until the end of the operation Josh has in mind.

"Make sure you don't fall asleep while I am inside the rental," Josh says to him.

"Yes, sir."

Josh is afraid Bhavany might be on her porch swatting mosquitoes. "If the old lady gets suspicious and comes out with lantern in her hand, what do you do?"

"I am supposed to persuade her not to call cops." "Good man!"

Josh enters the rental after making sure Bhavany isn't around, He carries a tool kit containing accessories needed for a break-in, including a high-power flashlight to be wrapped around his forehead.

Using heavy-duty punch pliers, he cuts the lock and gets in. He closes the door softly and turns on the headlight. His plan is to get inside the attic. The staircase creaks as he climbs up the stairs. He tiptoes to keep it quiet. He reaches the inclined attic door. The attic has been kept locked by a very old lock, the same lock Thoma used in 1975. Josh realizes there is no need to use heavy-duty pliers to cut it. Rust has mostly eaten it. He pulls it loose. It crumbles in his hands. He tosses it, opens the attic door, and ease inside.

"Hey, you!"

Josh hits the roof at the unexpected voice. He looks around and then up. Staring down at him is Chettiar's skull, whatever is remaining of it.

Moths have eaten most of it. "You owe me rent," it says.

Its teeth clack. Two gaping holes replace his eyes. He lost his left eye to Subashini's attack following his rape of the saintly Ann. Even though it was closed off ever since, it is now open for business. Josh reaches out and lifts the skull off the hook Thoma used to hang it the night before the family's exodus. He carries it, eases out of the attic, closes the attic door, and climbs down the staircase. He deposits the skull in a large plastic bag he brought with him.

It is half past one in the morning. There is half an hour left before two, the critical time when a young woman would be murdered. He needs to hurry. He turns off the flashlight around his head, gets out of the rental, and rushes to the waiting cab.

"Take me to the bridge," Josh says after waking up the cabby who had promised not to fall asleep.

When he reaches the bridge, there is a huge crowd there. They are all over the riverbanks as if it is a festival. Police are everywhere to control them. The officials huddle under the bridge and wait for the critical hour when a twenty-one-year-old woman's body would arrive.

Monsoon Man parks one block from the bridge. Josh walks to the riverbank carrying the heavy bag. In the taxi, he had attached the skull to a heavy rock and deposited it in the bag, securely sealing it with duct tape.

Fifteen minutes left! When he reaches the riverbank, he hurls the package into the river. The river swallows it. It is five minutes to the hour.

"Now, go and rest in peace," Josh says to the skull. "Go and find your body, glue yourself to it, and live happily ever after. Don't you ever murder this town's young women again."

Ringing in his mind is the loud memory of the contents of the 1975 letter from home to Canada, which said that Thoma performed a half-burial of Chettiar by throwing his body inside the river while Thalli carried his head back to the rental. After a long separation, the head and the body are reunited to stay married—until probably death would do them part? That should keep Chettiar's disturbed soul, if he has a soul, out of distress.

Burial is now complete. Josh undid the thirty-eight-year-old curse on Chettiar.

While sitting in the hotel lobby early the next morning and waiting for the cab to take him to the airport, Josh sips coffee and removes the rubber loop around the folded copy of *Mannuthy Chronicles*. The paper was left in front of his room as a courtesy of the hotel.

He is alone in the lobby. A female receptionist clad in a green sari sits at the hotel counter some fifty feet away. She yawns and swats mosquitoes with a magazine. The white blades of many ceiling fans in the lobby spin lazily, making whirring sounds like giant tropical flies.

Josh slowly opens the newspaper and looks at the front page. There is a news item in bold letters on the front page. It catches his attention. He reads:

Mannuthy citizens assembled under the notorious Mannuthy Municipal Bridge last night have no supernatural story to tell. As you all know, the night belonged to the September full moon. The crowd was expecting to see the usual spectacle they had been seeing previous years. The clock struck the crucial hour of 2 AM. To their surprise, they did not see a twenty-one-year-old woman's strangled body brought to the bridge to be hung under it by an invisible hangman. She used to be hung on the reinforced concrete beam by her trademark long hair.

Josh realizes that he is the only person in the whole wide world who knows the secret behind the newspaper story. Only he knows who executed a certain midnight operation to stop the massacre.

"Your taxi is ready, sir."

Josh jumps at the abrupt announcement and drop the paper. He didn't know the cabby sneaked behind him. He stands up, waking up to the reality that he needs to get in the cab and head out to the airport. He turns around to greet the cabbie.

There is no cabbie there.

Josh knows better. He gets up and follows the invisible cabby, who carries his suitcases. Will Monsoon Man take another detour, taking him to some supernatural location far from the airport? He hopes not.

"Take me straight to the airport this time, you hear?" Josh says. There is no reply.

The sari-clad receptionist looks up from the magazine and screams in alarm at seeing two suitcases floating and moving forward in front of Josh.

She then looks oddly at Josh because he is talking to the suitcases.

THIRTEEN

THE ATTIC

As Josh steps out of the hotel lobby with Monsoon Man, his phone rings. He fishes it out of pocket. It is his travel agent, Balan. "Houston, we have a problem," says Balan. "What now?"

"Sir, there is a mix-up with your reservation. Your flight is not today, as was planned. It is one week from now. Sorry."

"Sorry doesn't cut it. How did this happen?"

"Airline dropped the ball. They messed up the reservation. My travel agency is clean."

"I don't care who is at fault; I am in trouble now." "Very good, sir."

"Don't say *very good*. This is bad, very bad." "Very good, sir."

Josh heads back to his room after renewing hotel reservation for another week. He is worried he could be stranded in Kerala leaving the Canadian flight a possibility when stars align.

While riding up to his thirteenth-floor room, something happens.

Mannuthy rental's attic appears in front of him. The attic has teleported to the hotel. The attic wall is right there staring at him.

The wall has been witnessing Chettiar's skull all these years. The skull disappeared one day ago.

The wall is bare. Or is it? He stares closely and sees a door outline on the wall.

Is it a trapdoor?

"You are on the thirteenth floor, sir," the elevator attendant says.

Josh walks out from the elevator down the hallway heading to his room, 1313. He continues to see the door outline in front of him. Suddenly, the outline disappears, and an opening emerges. He halts and peers at the opening.

There is a tunnel the door opens to.

"May I help you, sir?" the housecleaning lady asks. Josh realizes he had stopped in the hallway and is staring in front of him. The attic scene disappears the moment the janitor speaks. Josh resumes his walk.

Josh is certain that the tunnel he saw ends in a dark place. What is it that he saw there? Something or someone was there.

When he gets inside his room, the scene reappears. The tunnel is back in vision. The figure at its end looks more like an animal than a human.

Look, look! Look closely, an inner voice screams at Josh. He does.

An ominous-looking face in charcoal-black reveals itself. It laughs in a high-pitched squealing sound.

Thalli, is that you? He is sure that it's her face that he sees and it's her laughter that he hears. What is she doing in the attic?

There is someone else behind her, someone vaguely familiar. Josh looks closely, but then the vision disappears.

Josh concentrates on his mind's eye, frantically trying to retrieve the image of whoever is behind Thalli. Must be someone important. Who is it?

The only way to disentangle the mystery is to make another trip to the rental and explore its attic—Another secretive investigation in the middle of the night is called for. Josh is disinclined to such an adventure. Once is enough; twice, he could be caught. A second attempt at the break-in spells trouble.

However, something propels him toward it, even if he might be thrown into a Kerala slammer, delaying his return to Canada.

He is certain he cannot help being seiged by horror. Its six letters dance in front of him wearing hideous masks. He isn't up to handling the task alone. He needs a partner in crime.

Josh lets himself inside the Wi-Fi room in the hotel lobby. He googles his classmates from Kerala University. The name *Devan* shows up prominently. Josh is delighted to realize his close friend and classmate is still living in Mannuthy. He and Wilma were lovers.

Devan stands out among Josh's friends, not only because they attended classes together but also because he would have become his brother-in-law if his love affair with Wilma bloomed into marriage. She disappeared on her twenty-first birthday without a trace.

Josh follows up his Google inquiry with a visit to his friend. They meet up at Devan's house.

"It is bizarre that my attempts to get to the airport in time fizzled in outlandish ways," Josh says. "There is something gripping about the events causing multiple delays in getting to my destination; it is as if they are preordained."

He narrates recent episodes. "Look, cabbie was tossed out of the cab on our way to airport, Monsoon Man drove me to Amballore home instead of airport, I was compelled to bury Thoma under the legendary coconut palm at Amballore home causing delay in my trip, and I was side-tracked to join Ann to visit Mannuthy rental. Bhavany's narration of September full-moon massacre led me to skip travel plans to put a stop to the annual murder tragedy in Mannuthy. And now, my attic vision prompts me to take further action, dragging me deeper into a widening mess."

Suddenly, a flash of recollection overpowers Josh. "Yes, yes, it was Wilma!!!"

Devan is lost. "What are you saying, Josh? Have you gone off your rocker?"

"The one behind Thalli in my attic vision is a she and she is Wilma!" Josh says excitedly.

Devan remembers the last day when he met Wilma at her home to celebrate her twenty-first birthday. It was a full-moon night. "You know, I would have married her at the drop of a hat," Devan says. "I still love her, even after my marriage."

"That is what I call love," Josh says.

"The night I was with her—the night she disappeared—was special. The love I felt when we strolled under the full moon was special. She had a garland made of Jasmine flowers wrapped around her beautiful hair. We strolled the grounds of your rental hand in hand, bathing in the soft moonlight, with no care in the world, and on top of the world.

"Why did she disappear on me?" Devan looks anguished. He starts talking to Wilma, his gaze fixed far away. "Wilma, hon, was the outpouring of joy we shared that night the calm before the storm? Where are you now? I want to see you again, be near you, and hold your hand. Please come back!"

Josh is surprised to see tears on a grownup man.

Devan stands up, walks down the room, unlocks the bottom drawer of a wooden cabinet, and pulls out a book and reads from it:

Emerald green meadows glisten
Dews glitter in sunrise
I know you and I are those dews
Hugging each other in love's madness

"Your sister, Wilma, penned this," Devan says. "This is the book of poems she wrote."

"I can hardly believe she was a poet," Josh says. "She was quiet like church mouse."

Josh reads some verses and notes that there are no poems after what Devan read.

"Sure, there is none," Devan says. "It is the last poem she penned. She wrote it while we strolled on the very last night I spent with her."

Josh resumes reading some previous verses.

Let me love you from sunrise to sunset
And beyond when stars fill the sky
Let me love you again from next sunrise
Down to the very last day of my life

"How prescient!" says Josh. "Did my sister have premonition that it was her last day?"

"I have been asking myself the very same question all these years," Devan says.

I'll live after death 'cause love keeps me alive

I'll love after death 'cause my love's immortal
I'll wait for you at end of tunnel in darkness
Wishing for light when I meet you again

"*'End of tunnel in darkness!' Imagine that! That* is the tunnel I saw in my vision," Josh says. "She must have had foreboding of some impending disaster."

"We got engaged on our last day together," Devan reveals. "When and where?" Josh is unaware of this news.

"During the birthday celebration, just after she recited the poem to me," Devan says. "We were alone, but the stars in the sky bore witness. I adorned her pretty finger with engagement ring and then I kissed her; my first kiss."

He takes a deep breath and continues. "Even though she sounded happy the whole time I was with her, I got the feeling that something was eating her."

"I feel my vision is telling me something," Josh says. "It is begging me to disclose something to the world, something gruesome that happened in the darkness."

"I agree there is meaning to the tunnel and what you saw at its end," Devan says. "I get the feeling you need to be careful. I am getting vibes there is danger lurking under the triplex roof."

Devan's car pulls up across from the rental at midnight. For the second night in a row, Bhavany is not on her front porch. Lights are out inside her house and the landlord's. Josh thanks his lucky stars.

"Are you sure you don't have second thoughts about this?" Devan confirms Josh's heart and soul is with the mission.

"I won't chicken out now," Josh says.

They sneak into the rental under night's cover, hauling the tools with them. The front door is not locked; Josh cut the lock previous night. After cautiously closing the door behind them, they fit their foreheads with the headlights and turn them on. The room is lit brightly. They climb the stairs, Josh in the lead and Devan in tow. The door at the top of the stairs let them into the attic. Devan makes sure the spring-loaded door doesn't slam behind them.

They approach the wall Josh saw in his vision and search for a rectangular outline.

"Turn on the other headlight," Josh says.

Devan directs a handheld searchlight toward the wall. They take closer looks. Josh taps around the wall. There is no door outline.

"Take iPhone photo and play with resolution or zoom it," Devan says.

Josh takes pictures at various angles while Devan directs the searchlight. He zooms the pictures. They see a faint rectangle made visible through the worn-out painting. It is the trapdoor they are looking for!

The outline is cleverly meshed into the wall, making it indistinguishable under fresh paint. The flow of time ate away part of the painting. It still requires a high-resolution picture to see it, or to see through it.

Josh pushes on the trapdoor. It doesn't budge. He uses all his might and tries again. Still, no response. "Give me a hand, will you?" Josh asks Devan.

The sustained push by the two men finally does the trick. The heavy concrete door protests with a loud creaking sound and parts ways with the wall. The trapdoor is made with reinforced concrete, just like the wall. Now they are staring into a dark opening.

"The door is at least one foot thick," Devan estimates.

They figure it is five feet tall by two feet wide. It rests on four heavy-duty steel hinges, each of which is half a foot long, half a foot wide, and one inch thick. These hinges give the concrete door enough support to withstand collapse due to its own weight.

As the door opens all the way out, their headlights illuminate Bhavany's roof, revealing a passage in front of them. There are tall walls on the entire triplex roof.

The door has a heavy stainless-steel bar attached to its outside. This enables one to pull it open from outside. Josh and his family knew that Bhavany's unit did not have an attic. Their knowledge proves to be right—no attic is found above her unit. The family thought that their attic was a self-standing structure, unattached to any other unit. The discovery of a trapdoor disproves that assumption.

They tiptoe to avoid waking up Bhavany and walk to the end of the open space. This open space appeared to Josh in his vision as a dark tunnel. He now realizes that it is more like a passage than a tunnel.

A face stare at them!

"Good god! who is it?" Devan asks, grabbing the knife in his pocket. "Don't stab," Josh says. "Not yet."

They look at the face closely. A gigantic head sits on the floor with its devilish face staring at them with fiery eyes. The teeth are bared. It is statue of Bhadrakali.

The Hindu goddess who killed the demon king Asura gazes at them. Her eight arms are sprawled around her midnight-colored face, and one arm holds Asura's butchered head. The face is so dark that it would be invisible but for the high-intensity flashlight Devan carries. The statue's neck and lower body are absent. The head is the same size as the attic, as large as a living quarter, measuring eight feet tall, twenty feet wide (all the way from the front to the back of the triplex), and ten feet deep. It spans the top of Chettiar's house. Bhadrakali is hidden from the outside because tall walls surround it. They walk around the statue. There are foot-wide clearings around the statue, beyond which walls take over and roof ends.

"It is this face that I saw in my vision, and I thought it was Thalli," Josh says. "As you know, Thalli is the goddess's incarnation and they resemble each other."

"How can anyone scale the tall walls and get to the roof from outside?

It is impossible," says Devan.

"Take a look around you," Josh says and shines the flashlight toward the tall palm trees surrounding the triplex. The clever designer of the imposing roof counted on the tall trees to gain access to the roof!

"So, this is the mystery at the end of the tunnel; a dark face!" Devan says, pointing to the statue. He puts back the drawn knife.

"Not quite. There is more or should be!" Josh says. Devan looks at him curiously. Josh doesn't elaborate. "Where is Wilma you saw in your vision?" Devan asks.

"That, my friend, is the one-million-rupee question," Josh says.

They examine the enormous statue. During his stay at the rental, Josh didn't know of its existence; neither did anyone else, as far as he knows.

"There is a prominent hook on Bhadrakali's nose," Devan notes. "A giant nose ring!"

Josh finds out that it is not a nose ring after all, it is a hook. Tied to the hook is a metallic chain. The chain wraps around her head, going behind it.

It then loops through another hook. When someone pulls on the chain, Bhadrakali's mouth opens, granting access to its interior! Clever idea!

They note that the weather-beaten chain has almost disintegrated due to rust.

"Do we have any rope with us?" Josh asks.

They search the toolbox. Fortunately, there is a heavy-duty steel-braided nylon rope inside. Devan takes out the rope and replaces the disintegrated chain with it. He ties its one end to the nose hook and threads it through the back hook. They pull hard on the rope. No response.

"Let us hang from the rope together," Devan says. They attach a metal bar to rope's end, and this enables both to hang simultaneously to apply added force on the rope.

They together hang from the rope with their feet dangled in the air. They hear loud cranking-creaking sound, like an elephant's trumpet roar. The goddess's mouth opens, landing both men on the floor.

They go around to statue's front. A huge gaping mouth greets them. It is a twenty-foot-wide opening. The statue wall is easily one foot thick. Its thick reinforced-concrete walls make it a formidable fortress. The interior is as big as Thoma's attic, big enough to have bedroom, kitchen, and bathroom.

They cautiously step inside her mouth. Pungent air greets them. Spiders crawl.

Then they see it. Hanging from the ceiling of the goddess is a human skeleton. Devan directs light toward it. The ribs and some bones have fallen off, leaving just the bare bones of a skeleton.

"Wilma!" Josh shouts at the top of his voice.

"Wilma? My Wilma?" Devan asks incredulously, staring at the skeleton.

"Exactly. It can't be anyone else. It is my sister, and your love. That is who she is." Josh says excitedly but sadly.

Devan continues to stare with unbelieving eyes, trying to remember the face that drummed with life once upon a time. "My love," he murmurs faintly, and his voice sinks. "All these years, you were hiding inside the goddess's mouth, my darling!"

He hugs the skeleton tenderly. Tears trickle down. "How did you die, my darling?" Devan continues to talk.

Just at that moment, skeleton's right ring finger bone breaks loose and crashes onto the floor. Josh picks it up. Loosely fitting the bone and wrapping around it is a gold ring. Both men look at it in the headlight.

Inscribed on it in tiny letters is "To Wilma From Devan."

Josh remembers the frantic search he and his family conducted at the time Wilma disappeared forty years ago in 1973. Their search ended up with no leads.

"The fortress-like structure of the goddess diminished the stench from the dead body, and this explains why the murder was concealed," Josh says more to the world than to Devan.

"Murder? Or suicide?" Devan asks.

Josh retrieves the skeleton from the ceiling, collect all the fallen bones, and deposits them inside a large plastic bag.

"As soon as I saw the trapdoor in my vision, I suspected that Wilma was abducted through it," Josh says. "If so, it was murder, not suicide."

They bury Wilma in the waters under the Mannuthy Municipal Bridge. It is Josh's second water burial in two days.

FOURTEEN

THE WEREWOLF DYNASTY

"I shall be Dr. Watson, you be Sherlock Holmes," Devan says to Josh.

They meet at Devan's house the next day, rested after a good sleep following the night of adventure.

"Who killed Wilma, Sherlock?" Devan asks.

"Jaygust is the first suspect," Josh says. "He is known as cradle strangler. He tried to strangle Kareena, with no success. He is a suspect in the strangling death of Rafeena. If we follow this trail, it leads to the inevitable conclusion that he is behind Wilma's death."

"Is that it? No twists in the plot? Just a simple story?" Devan is skeptical.

"It is anything but simple," Josh assures. "There are twists galore and turns galore."

"I am all ears, Holmes," Devan says.

"Let us start with Rafeena," Josh says. "Police believed an insider killed her because the girls' bedroom door was intact. An outside culprit was counted out, even though they couldn't prove it. Family suspected that Jaygust did it, who slept in the attic above the bedroom, giving him easy access. He didn't have to break in. He has history of violent behavior when he transmutes to werewolf."

"There is a hole in the theory," Devan says. "What if the crime was committed by one of the girls? Say Thalli, who could have committed the murder in one of her supernatural fits, during transformation to Bhadrakali?"

"Thalli transforms to Bhadrakali only under special circumstances, like when she is threatened or provoked," Josh says. "For example, she transmuted when Chettiar attacked her under the bridge. Rafeena was such a simple girl she couldn't even hurt a fly, leave alone provoke Thalli to turn her into a killer goddess."

"So Jaygust killed her?"

"Not so fast! Logic or evidence-based analysis would blame Jaygust until yesterday when we discovered the trapdoor."

"Elaborate, please."

"Let us start with Rafeena.

"There are two reasons why Chettiar didn't kill Rafeena. The first has to do with the nature of the killing. The killer attacked Rafeena savagely. It was an uncontrolled, no-holds-barred attack. There was no attempt to conceal evidence like getting rid of the body; her strangled and disfigured body was practically begging to reveal that it was an animal attack or a werewolf attack."

"That makes both Chettiar and Jaygust culprits—father-son team of werewolves."

"Not so. There are subtle differences between Chettiar and Jaygust when they turn into werewolves. It is true both can commit murder under the grip of supernatural transformation on full-moon nights.

"When Jaygust undergoes metamorphosis, he becomes a maniac. A primitive, raw impulse takes over to mangle, strangle, and kill. He is under siege of an evil so overpowering that premeditation and planning don't apply to him."

"Well, werewolf attacks are not orderly by nature, and Chettiar isn't exception."

"On the contrary, Chettiar is different! His actions in werewolf state are controlled, measured, and planned.

"Example is the rape of Ann. There was premeditation on his part. He finished his deplorable act and managed to get out safely, taking exit by trapdoor. Sense doesn't seem to take leave of him in werewolf state, unlike Jaygust."

"What you are saying is that there is method to Chettiar's madness," Devan says. "But there is only madness to Jaygust's methods."

They laugh.

Devan continues. "You're proposing a theory based upon circumstantial evidence to point a finger at Jaygust. We need objective evidence."

"Well, you're asking for it; so here it is.

"Jaygust had bloodstains on him the day of Rafeena's murder—I noticed it; our family noticed it. We urged him to shower, and this got rid of the stains and police was left with no objective evidence to nail him. I didn't reveal it to Kareena when I phoned her that morning in case line was tapped."

"Let us get to Wilma," Devan says. "You saw Thalli and Wilma together in your vision. Did Thalli murder Wilma and hang her in Bhadrakali suite?"

"My vision was unsettling, to say the least. It brought to the top of my memory Thalli's transmutation to Bhadrakali under Mannuthy bridge upon Chettiar's attempt to rape her and the ensuing murder. I thought Thalli killed Wilma, even though I was baffled by how a decent girl like Wilma could provoke Thalli. I discovered during last night's triplex roof exploration that it wasn't Thalli who appeared in my vision but Bhadrakali, who resembles Thalli."

"You mean to say that since Wilma was hung inside the Bhadrakali suite, they appeared together in your vision."

"Exactly."

"It still doesn't absolve Thalli of the crime."

"Thalli couldn't have. Wilma couldn't have provoked her to transform to a killer. Let us still be skeptics and think Thalli killed Wilma. The way it could have played out is for Thalli to become Bhadrakali, cut off Wilma's head, hold the spoils in one of her eight arms, and sit in a lotus meditation position in a trance. But Wilma's head wasn't cut off, as attested by last night's discovery."

"It could be Jaygust who hauled Wilma to the roof," Devan says. "Jaygust did nothing to Wilma."

"Explain to me, oh Guru." Devan's eyes shine with intrigue.

"I say this for two reasons," Josh says. "First, Jaygust is unaware of the existence of the trapdoor that leads to Bhadrakali. Second, he slept through the tragedy. If he were awake, he would have become werewolf—it was a full-moon night, don't forget—and he would have killed Wilma instantly in a horrifically graphic manner. But he would have left the body right where he killed her: in the bedroom. He couldn't have had patience to carry her anywhere."

"Why was he unaware of the trapdoor?"

"It was a secret known only to Chettiar. I promise I'll come to it."

"What if Jaygust was an accomplice? What if he opened the door for an outsider, say Chettiar or someone else, to kidnap her and closed the door after the intruder left?"

"Very good analysis, Watson," Josh says. "It would explain why the room wasn't broken into and yet crime was committed.

"If Jaygust had woken up during the night of Wilma's disappearance, he would have transformed to werewolf, making him too unpredictable to be a reliable partner in crime," Josh says. "This discounts theory of collaboration."

"Our discovery of trapdoor opens the door to just one possibility—Chettiar abducted Wilma," Devan says.

"My turn to say 'exactly,'" Josh says.

"Describe to me how Chettiar committed the crime," Devan says.

"Well, I have been turning in my mind events of that horrific night when Wilma disappeared. After our discovery last night, I am convinced that what I am going to tell you is the only thing that could have happened." Josh tells him what happened.

When the midnight clock struck on Wilma's birthday. The loud music of the birthday party had already subsided and there was an eerie silence.

Chettiar is sleeping in his unit with his wife by the side. He is aware there was a loud birthday party at Thoma's unit to which he wasn't invited. He moves his wife's hair from his face, and sits up in the bed.

The fragrance! Where is it coming from? Jasmine flower's intoxicating fragrance overpowers him. He looks out through the window and an instant transformation overtakes him when he sees the full moon. His skin turns dark, long brown-grey hair protrudes from under the skin and fills his body, and claws grow at the fingertips. He looks like a wolf.

He jumps, shoots through the air, pulls open the bedroom door and gets out. Out in the open, he stares at the full moon and howls. His sense of smell swells dramatically. He moves rapidly, sniffing the air, and making snorting sounds like a pig.

The fragrance pulls him like a magnet. He can no longer stand it. He climbs the tall coconut palm rapidly, reaches the top in no time, and jumps onto the wall surrounding Bhadrakali and down to the roof. The fragrance pulls him toward Thoma's attic. As he approaches the attic wall, the fragrance became unbearable. He pulls on the trapdoor with a wild force.. The wall opens in a split second. He gets in.

He tramples on his sleeping son, Jaygust, and pauses. He takes a closer look; a vague awareness comes over his face, but still can't place the stranger sleeping in the attic, is sure he has seen him somewhere. He continues to move forward, and opens the attic door.

He pauses at the top of the stairs, gazes at the sleeping girls, and climbs down. Now he sees the long hair of a girl, interlaced with Jasmine garland. She is in the group of the girls. He picks her up. She shrieks. He swiftly muffles the scream by closing her mouth shut with his fiercely strong hands.

"I'll kill you if you scream."

She faints. He carries her upstairs. He takes her out of the attic, and closes the trapdoor. He carries her into Bhadrakali's mouth and closes the demon goddess' mouth.

"Why did you say only Chettiar knew of the existence of the Bhadrakali suite?" Devan asks.

"The way it looked last night is a telltale sign that the roof and its anomalous architecture have not been touched in long time," Josh says. "Wilma had been hanging for a long time. No one had entered the roof since Chettiar died. Chettiar had kept it a closely guarded secret."

"Why the secrecy?"

"Bhadrakali suit is a living quarter, a secret abode where Chettiar concealed and housed the kidnapped victims, raped them, and made them pregnant."

"You mean Wilma wasn't killed on the day she was abducted?"
"Exactly."

Devan looks agonized, imagining the slavery that Chettiar imposed on Wilma, his love.

"How long was she alive, you think?" Devan asks.

"Most probably until the end of her pregnancy. He replaced his victims with fresh twenty-one-year-old females."

"Even after he died!" Devan can't help saying his line of thought. "There's a difference. September full-moon murders under the bridge were the work of a disturbed soul; the kidnapping of twenty-one-year-old women while he was alive was to perpetuate his dynasty."

"What is the significance of twenty-one-year-old women?"

"Maybe Chettiar believed that such an age is the prime of youth. He was looking for the most fertile soil to sow his seed."

"Where is the baby? There was only Wilma's skeleton we saw last night."

"Chettiar must have had contacts in town or elsewhere where babies were brought up. He was on a mission—produce a generation of werewolves."

"It is a wild theory."

"I'll prove to you it isn't so."

Devan's face is lit with surprise and intrigue. "I can hardly wait to get the proof. On a different matter, did Chettiar plant Jaygust at your home to destroy Thoma?"

"Most possibly," Josh says. "Chettiar was very vengeful. He hated Thoma and Ann and wanted to destroy them. Jaygust was an agent Chettiar created to wreak havoc in Thoma's life."

"Maybe Chettiar schemed to carry the fight right into your home by planting Jaygust." Devan suggests. "Jaygust rebelled against Thoma, joined forces with his younger siblings to form *Gang of Four*, and turned them against their father."

"Thoma deserved better," Josh said. "After he was expelled from his ancestral home, he shouldn't have gone to Mannuthy. It was like going from frying fan into fire."

"It looks as if fate declared open season on Thoma," Devan says. "Yes, Thoma was the target of fate's ire," Josh says. "But there were redeeming factors that should make his soul peaceful. He had a saintly wife, Ann, and loving elder children."

That afternoon, Josh, and Devan board a helicopter belonging to *Skywalker Helicopter Tours* in Trichur. They hire it for an afternoon flight to Mannuthy and back.

Flying over Mannuthy skies, they see the roofs of some buildings hosting the dark statue of Bhadrakali. A peculiar architectural feature is noticeable—the statues have high walls surrounding them, as if to conceal the demon goddess from the public's eye. The statues are visible only while flying.

"Inside each of the scattered Bhadrakali mouths, a certain twenty-one- year-old woman's skeleton is hanging," Josh says to Devan. "There are many Wilmas down there."

Devan did not turn back to Josh to reply. He was deeply absorbed in staring at the surreal scene.

Jose Thekkumthala is the author of the critically acclaimed novel *Amballore House*. The author received his PhD in nuclear physics from the University of Alberta, Canada.

He is currently working as a Medical Physicist in the field of radiation therapy for cancer patients.

He enjoys hiking, soccer, chess, and reading.

He lives with his wife, Jennifer, and their beautiful daughters, Lisa and April.

GLOSSARY OF TERMS

Beedi	An Indian cigarette
Chatta	A white cotton jacket worn by Kerala Christian women
Dosa	Pancake made from fermented rice and lentil batter
Idli	Cake made by steaming rice flour and fermented black lentil
Toddy	An alcoholic beverage, or toddy, made in Kerala; it is also known as coconut-palm wine
Kanji	Boiled rice with starch water
Kerala	A state in India famous for its natural beauty
Lakh	One hundred thousand
Mahavishnu	A Hindu god
Mahout	A person who rides an elephant
Malayalam	The official language spoken in Kerala
Mundu	A white cotton garment that is draped around the waist; it is worn mostly by men and some women in Kerala

Namaste	Respectful form of greeting in Hindu custom; namaste is spoken with a slight bow with palms pressed together, fingers pointing upward, and thumbs close to the chest
Pala	An evergreen tropical tree belonging to the family *Apocynaceae*; it is also called the Indian devil tree
Parasuraman	Creator of Kerala
Puja	Worship
Popadam	A thin, circular, flattened cornmeal cake fried in oil
Sambar	Lentil-based vegetable stew in tamarind broth

REFERENCES

1   William Wordsworth, "Preface to the Second Edition of the Lyrical Ballads," in *English Romantic Writers*, 2nd ed (New York: Harcourt, 1995), 425.

2   http://www.wikihow.com/Cite-the-Bible-/Image:Cite-the-Bible-Step-16- Version-2.jpg.

3   William Shakespeare, *The Tempest*, edited by Virginia M. Vaughan and Alden T. Vaughan (175 Fifth Avenue/3rd Floor, New York, NY 10010: Bloomsbury Academic & Professional, 2000).

4   Pitts Theology Library Archives and Manuscripts. John Henry Newman Papers. 1836–64. n.d. MSS 100.

5   http://www.lyrics.com/lyric/356782.

6   en.proverbia.net › Authors › E.

7   Lao-tzu, www.verybestquotes.com.

8   Thomas Gray, *Elegy Written in a Country Churchyard* (London: Sampson Low, Son, and Marston, 1869).

9   Charles, Dickens, *A Tale of Two Cities* (New York: New American Library, 1963).

10   Frank L. Baum, *The Wonderful Wizard of Oz* (New York: George M. Hill, 1900).

11   William Shakespeare, *The Tragedy of Hamlet, Prince of Denmark*, vol. XLVI, in *The Harvard Classics* (New York: P. F. Collier & Son, 1909–14).

12   William Shakespeare, *The Tragedy of Macbeth*, vol. XLVI, in *The Harvard Classics* (New York: P. F. Collier & Son, 1909–14).

13   William Shakespeare, *As You Like It* (London: Oxford University Press, 1914).

14   William Shakespeare, *King Lear* (London: Oxford University Press, 1914).

15   John Donne, *The Complete Poetry and Selected Prose of John Donne* (Random House Publishing Group, January 1978), ISBN 0394604407.